"History is making this decision for us. People think rulers rule, but we are ruled by precedent and necessity and duty. There are perks. The royal chest can buy you all the nice things you want. Every physical need you have will be amply met from now on. What is unaffordable to me, however, and to *you*, is choice. We are bound by duty to the crown."

"You might be. But I'm not you. I'm not bound by your ruler or rules. I'm not..."

"Lexi. Stop upsetting yourself. It's done. Unless that paternity test comes back with a different answer, we started down this path in Paris. There is no fork in the road now."

"But..."

"I know." He came close enough to cup her cheek and set the pad of his thumb against her trembling mouth. "Believe me when I say I know exactly how you feel. And you put up a good fight. I admire you for it. It reassures me that you'll weather what's coming. But save your strength for other fights, because this one is over. We're marrying."

Canadian **Dani Collins** knew in high school that she wanted to write romance for a living. Twenty-five years later, after marrying her high school sweetheart, having two kids with him, working at several generic office jobs and submitting countless manuscripts, she got The Call. Her first Harlequin novel won the Reviewers' Choice Award for Best First in Series from *RT Book Reviews*. She now works in her own office, writing romance.

Books by Dani Collins

Harlequin Presents

Innocent in Her Enemy's Bed
Awakened on Her Royal Wedding Night
Marrying the Enemy
Husband for the Holidays

Four Weddings and a Baby

Cinderella's Secret Baby
Wedding Night with the Wrong Billionaire
A Convenient Ring to Claim Her
A Baby to Make Her His Bride

Bound by a Surrogate Baby

The Baby His Secretary Carries
The Secret of Their Billion-Dollar Baby

Diamonds of the Rich and Famous

Her Billion-Dollar Bump

Visit the Author Profile page
at Harlequin.com for more titles.

HIS HIGHNESS'S
HIDDEN HEIR

DANI COLLINS

Harlequin

PRESENTS

Harlequin®
PRESENTS™

ISBN-13: 978-1-335-93933-3

His Highness's Hidden Heir

Harlequin Enterprises ULC
22 Adelaide St. West, 41st Floor
Toronto, Ontario M5H 4E3, Canada
www.Harlequin.com

Printed in Lithuania

Recycling programs for this product may not exist in your area.

HIS HIGHNESS'S
HIDDEN HEIR

To you, Dear Reader, for loving romance and reading mine and making this, my 60th Harlequin, possible. Thank you!

CHAPTER ONE

THE ADAGE THAT SAID *If you want something done right, do it yourself* defined Lexi Alexander's twenty-five years of life.

Unfortunately, there were some things she simply couldn't do. For instance, she couldn't be famous and also be her own security detail.

Quietly cursing under her breath, she dismissed Nishan, the bodyguard her brother had hired, and left for the ballroom alone.

Poor Nishan hadn't meant to contract food poisoning. She knew that. Hadley was the real problem. Her brother had hired a man who hadn't been up to the task of protecting her even before he'd lost his lunch. Nishan hadn't known how to navigate her through the airports or the streets of Paris and there'd been a very un-reassuring alarm in his eyes as they'd run the gauntlet of paparazzi from the car to the hotel. He had allowed stylists to come and go from her room all afternoon without checking their bags. Now Lexi was without an escort as she joined the queue in the corridor, inching their way toward the ballroom.

She was perfectly safe, she reassured herself. The

hotel was in a type of lockdown, given the guest list for this gala included muckety-mucks from across Europe. It wasn't as though she wore millions of dollars in jewels the way she used to when attending something like this. Her fall from grace two years ago meant she'd had to call in a favor to rent one of last year's gowns, and her jewelry was costume. Very good costume, but costume nonetheless.

The bloom was so far off her rose, she half expected to be refused entry.

Which would break her, financially and emotionally. She had dropped funds she couldn't afford on the flight, the hotel and the plate fee of a five-figure donation benefiting war-injured children. She was hoping her attendance would polish out some of the tarnish on her reputation, but was really here to "bump into" one of the other guests, a French woman Lexi desperately wanted to direct her in an adaptation she was trying to get off the ground.

All of this was high-stakes gambling, something Lexi objected to in principle, but she had so few choices. Being famous since childhood meant she was perceived as rich and powerful. That made her a favorite target for paparazzi and others who were even less savory. She would love to get a job as a barista and live a quiet life above a bookstore, but that option wasn't available to her. She had cut back as much as she could, but she still needed an income that would pay the mortgage on her high-security mansion and allow her to keep her staff.

"Ms. Alexander." A young woman in a little black dress greeted her with a smile of recognition when Lexi arrived at the front of the line. It was the delighted smile Lexi had seen most of her life. The one that seemed to exclaim, *You're that girl from that show!*

The young woman's expression faltered, the way they all did these days, as she recalled the more recent headlines: Unapproved Ingredients. Chemical Burns. Class Action Lawsuit.

The young woman touched her earpiece and flashed Lexi a more sober look. "May I ask you to step to the side with me, please?"

No. Lexi kept her star-powered smile frozen in place. "Is there a problem?"

"Not at all. Only…" As they moved to the left of the entryway, the young woman looked back the way Lexi had come.

Lexi followed her gaze and watched all the people in their tuxedos and evening gowns, designer shoes and sparkling jewels, step toward the wall. Some bowed their heads.

She heard someone murmur, "Your Highness," right before a man—an absolute *Viking*—appeared.

He was tall, six four at least. He led his entourage like an invading party, ignoring everyone as he marched toward the ballroom, head high with his right to cut the line.

Maybe Lexi was supposed to lower her gaze, too, but she was too dazzled.

He wore a gorgeous tuxedo with a white jacket that hugged his broad shoulders. A sash of midnight blue was tucked beneath it, running diagonally from his left shoulder to his right hip where the silk protruded. It was pinned with a silver emblem shaped like a starburst. A row of medals sat in a line above his pocket square and a crest of some kind was embroidered on the pocket.

His dark blond hair was combed back from his forehead, revealing the rugged bone structure of his brow and cheeks and jaw. His nose was hawkish, his mouth wide and accentuated by his closely trimmed bronze beard.

All of that was mesmerizing enough, but his *eyes*. They were such a vivid blue, they made her shiver as his gaze slammed into hers while he approached.

He turned his head as he passed her, holding her gaze an extra second, never missing a step in his long, ground-eating stride.

Then she was staring at the pewter wolf's head that secured his long hair at his nape.

He melted into the crowded ballroom, taking all his dynamic energy with him, leaving a wake of rippling voices.

"Whew!" Lexi heard beside her. She had completely forgotten the young woman who was now blushing and fanning her face. "They told me to let him go by without stopping him. You can go in now. Thank you for waiting."

Lexi dragged her mind back to where she was and what she was supposed to be doing, but her thoughts were scattered like stars across the sky.

"Who, um, who is he?" she asked under her breath.

"Prince Magnus of Isleif."

"Of course." She pretended that meant something to her, but she was an American born in Scottsdale, Arizona. She'd been raised on film sets and didn't know much about the royals of Europe. Isleif was an island somewhere between Denmark and Greenland, if she recalled her online geography classes correctly. Otherwise, she knew nothing about it.

With a nod of thanks, she entered the busy ballroom.

She hated to enter a crowd alone. *I'm safe*, she affirmed to herself. The hotel had its own security in place and that young woman at the door was only letting in the approved guest list. These were all sophisticated people who cared very little for American actors turned failed online influencers.

But there had been some *terrible* posts over the years, especially after that most recent lawsuit.

She ignored the anxiety that tried to churn her belly and scanned the crowd, looking for her target, Bernadette Garnier.

Lexi wasn't short. She was five eight and wore five-inch heels, but it was still difficult to spot the director. The room lights were dimmed. Balloons floated above highboy tables and streamers draped from the ceiling. Clusters of people were shifting and pressing around the silent auction tables. More were jockeying at the bar. Waitstaff circulated, offering champagne.

She waved that off, moving closer to where an ensemble played a lively tune that was barely audible over the din of voices.

"Paisley!" A man close to her age brightened with discovery as she tried to excuse herself past him.

This was why she preferred to have a bodyguard with her.

"Guilty." Lexi forced a friendly smile and offered her hand. "My real name is Lexi Alexander."

Yes. My mother named me Alexandra Alexander, she often had to add.

"No, you're Paisley Pockets," he insisted. "My sister made me watch your show when we were kids." He leaned in to add in a tone that bordered on creepy, "Then I made her watch *Bungalow Bingo*."

This was typical from a man. *He* hadn't enjoyed a show about a girl who could travel in pockets, but he couldn't wait to brag about ogling her in her later work, when she'd worn short shorts and a bandeau.

"Can we get a photo?" He threw his arm around her and brought up his phone.

It was always more expedient to agree than protest that this was an invasion of her time and privacy, but damn Hadley for hiring such a green bodyguard. Who ate a shrimp-filled croissant from a street vendor's cart?

She smiled sunnily for the photo, experiencing a prickle of awareness as she did.

It took all her control to wait until the photo was taken before she glanced left, to where her inner radar was pulling her attention.

Prince Magnus was watching them. *Her.* He was tall enough he stood like a lighthouse amid the streaming crowd. As she held his stare, an itching sensation rose behind her breastbone, making the rest of her tingle.

The prince blinked once and glanced away, leaving her deflated at losing his attention.

"Darling." A woman arrived to grip her fan's arm, digging her nails into his sleeve.

"Look," he said with an excited wave at Lexi. "It's Paisley Pockets."

"Lexi Alexander. Hi." Lexi always offered her real name with her hand, even though she was resigned to having Paisley Pockets on her tombstone.

The woman offered a flat, dismissive smile. She ignored Lexi's hand and insisted to the man, "You need to meet my friend." She mumbled something in his ear.

The man shot Lexi a look and the tension in Lexi's belly twisted into a blistering knot.

That look was becoming familiar, too. *Don't speak to her. She's radioactive.*

"Excuse me," she said, even though they were already turning away.

This was why she was in Europe, taking long shots at finding work. No one in the American film industry would touch her.

You just have to stay in the game, her mother would say cheerfully, but Lexi was growing tired of the fight.

If she had other options she would take them, but this was all she had and the press loved to chum the waters with her old mistakes, making it impossible for her to outswim her past.

The next hour was a roller coaster of similar encounters. She wound her way around the auction items, bidding on the ones she knew she would lose since she couldn't afford any of them.

She didn't find Bernadette. Was she even here? People were still arriving, but she was very done with being here. This evening was starting to smell like a huge mistake.

The music paused for speeches. Lexi listened with half an ear, scanning the faces as best she could until she joined the polite applause. A gorgeous couple took to the dance floor in an elegant waltz.

"Shall we?" The deep, accented voice stirred the fine hairs near her ear while a wide, hot palm took possession of her hip.

She turned her head and her cheekbone grazed the silky whiskers of the Prince's chin. He essentially surrounded her, causing her heart to belatedly leap. She was snared. Caught. *Claimed.*

A dozen thoughts zipped through her mind—one of them that he couldn't possibly know who she was—but he was trailing his hand across her lower back, thumb grazing where her gown dipped to reveal her spine, leaving a spark of electricity against her skin.

He removed his touch and caught her hand, tugging her toward the dance floor.

It was as though a barbed hook in her chest pulled her to follow him, instantly painful yet impossible to resist.

He gathered her a little too close. Close enough that her legs brushed his as they moved, causing the silk lining of her gown to caress her thighs.

She knew how to dance, but she'd never moved so fluidly with anyone. Not without weeks of rehearsal. She was instantly in sync with him, her body giving over to his dominant lead with instinctive trust.

Don't, a protective voice warned. She'd learned the hard way that trust needed to be earned. Even then, it was conditional. She'd been hurt too many times to take anyone at face value, even a prince. What did he want? Sex?

"What's your name?" he asked in his accented English.

"You don't know?" She was genuinely surprised.

"Should I?"

"I'm Lexi Alexander, an actor from America." She didn't mention the cosmetic thing. "I would have thought someone on your team had recognized me." And warned him not to talk to her, let alone dance with her. People were noticing.

She glanced toward his entourage and saw a silver-haired man wearing an expression of subtle horror.

It wasn't funny, but she had a dark enough sense of humor to be amused.

"You didn't know who I was when you saw me," the prince chided. "I could tell by the way you looked at me."

"How was that?" She lifted her lashes, curious, and was instantly snared by the banked heat behind his startlingly blue irises.

"As a man."

Oh. Her heart lurched. He did want sex.

But maybe she did, too? A sensual weight seemed to land in her belly, one that emanated intense warmth through her torso, arriving in pinpoints at the tips of her breasts and between her thighs.

It was disconcerting enough to make her cheeks sting. She lowered her gaze, embarrassed at having such a visceral, obvious reaction.

"You're very beautiful." His voice deepened with admiration. Intimacy. "I couldn't help noticing you, too."

She knew she was judged to be beautiful. Hollywood told her that all the time, not that she believed her beauty was anything more than symmetrical features and above-average height. She did have genuinely nice hair, but the honey-gold streaks were placed there by her mother. Rhonda Alexander had trained in hair and makeup before Lexi was born, then treated her daughter as her own personal dress-up doll, an asset to be polished and shown off.

Thus, Lexi knew how to emphasize her eyes so they seemed bigger and shape her mouth into more of a sensual pout. She wore push-up bras and kept her weight audition-ready. Her nails were always manicured, her fashion choices edgy, but flattering.

"Beauty is in the eye of the beholder," she dismissed lightly.

"Aren't I the lucky one to be holding it." His mouth twitched. "You're here alone?"

"I am, but—" She gave a barely perceptible shake of her head, regretting that she had to rebuff him. It made her throat feel raw, but it was necessary. She was used often enough that she wouldn't do that to a stranger for a bit of positive press, no matter how badly she needed it.

The way his expression hardened told her he wasn't used to being refused what he wanted. And he wanted her. Not the way other men did, either. This was different. She understood that at a cellular level, as his hands subtly tightened on her. He wasn't intent on possessing a pretty object. No, this was elemental sexual desire—the kind she had never really experienced. She only recognized it in him because it was coming alive in her blood and nerve endings, sharpening her senses and filling her with craving.

Her heart tipped unsteadily in her chest. The pull toward him was so profound, the need to be near him so acute, it was terrifying. She wanted to fall into him and damn the consequences, which conversely made her want to run the other way out of self-protection.

"You need to t-talk to your people." She stopped dancing and pressed for him to release her.

He turned to stone, holding her in place without effort for three crashing heartbeats.

The strength in his arms was an iron cage, but he held her more with the pierce of his gaze. Then he dropped his touch and gave her a disinterested nod.

She had to do some of her best acting as he walked away, hiding how bereft she was as she moving in the opposite direction.

He left the gala moments later. She felt the energy in the room change. Maybe it was the awareness inside her that dimmed. Either way, she was dejected and swimming in loss.

She told herself it was because she hadn't managed to find Bernadette. She went back to the entrance of the ballroom and asked the greeter if the director had turned up.

The young woman checked her tablet. "It doesn't seem so."

Damn. Everything about this trip had become a complete waste of resources.

Lexi threw in the towel, unwilling to go back into the ballroom and face the growing stares. They were even more rude and speculative now that she'd danced with the prince.

He had probably wanted distance after being informed about her. She imagined he was furious that she'd compromised him.

For some reason that ate at her worse than the money she'd thrown away by coming here. Why? He was a total stranger. He meant nothing to her.

Yet she couldn't stop thinking about him as she made her way down the corridor to the elevators, worrying over their brief interaction like an abscessed tooth, poking at all the most painful aspects.

She had to keep an unbothered look on her face as she went. Small groups of people were chatting in alcoves and she had to step aside for another entourage of royals.

Wait. Was that—? It was!

Lexi was rarely starstruck, but she paused to watch Queen Claudine and her husband, King Felipe, continue toward the ballroom. Claudine had been a beauty contestant from New York, competing in Nazarine when she'd fallen in love with its crown prince. He had since ascended to the throne. Their courtship was straight out of a romance novel, the kind Lexi would love to develop into a movie and star in, not that she could touch Queen Claudine's natural beauty—

"Lexi!" a male voice called.

She glanced to the end of the corridor where it ended at the mezzanine. A man stood on the far side of the circular rail that looked onto the hotel's entrance foyer below. He lifted his camera to point it at her.

The paparazzi was roped off outside, but that wasn't just any photographer. Her heart nearly came out her throat as she recognized her stalker.

Instinctively, she pushed through the nearest door.

She had an impression of half a dozen men, including Prince Magnus, before someone grabbed her. Shock rendered her meager self-defense training useless. Her right arm was twisted into the middle of her back and her scream was still trapped in her throat when her face smacked into the wall.

CHAPTER TWO

MAGNUS THOROLF HAD already been in a foul mood when he arrived at this hotel. It was a version of the foul mood he'd been stewing in for the last fourteen years, ever since he'd been plucked from his training session on a ski hill in Norway and shuffled into a van by men in suits and sunglasses.

One blood test later, he was deemed the legitimate heir to the Isleif throne, something his mother could have told him at any time in the previous eighteen years of his life.

I was afraid they would take you away from me, she cried when the truth came out.

That was exactly what had happened.

His life, which at the time had been filled with endless possibility, had shrunk to duty and protocol and service to a crown he had no desire to wear.

Which suggested he didn't love Isleif, but that was the furthest thing from the truth. The best memories of his life were summers and Christmases at his mother's cottage in the windy island nation, chasing his brother and sister down a beach or across a snow-covered field.

He couldn't think of that time without a knife of nostalgia turning in him.

Ignorance really was bliss.

It certainly had been an hour ago, when a woman had snared his attention and he'd thought he might have amenable company in his bed tonight.

He wasn't even sure how or why she'd caught his eye. Yes, she was beautiful. Her blond hair was swept to the side, exposing one of her high cheekbones. Her pillowy lips were painted an earthy red, her eyeshadow bronze to match her gown.

The gown itself had been both elegant and sexy as hell. The silk had wrapped her throat then left her shoulders bare as it parted to cradle her ample breasts. It was fitted to her waist and hips, then fell open across one thigh, making the most of her stunning figure.

So, yes, she was easy to look at, but beautiful women made themselves available to him all the time, not that Magnus took full advantage of that small perk of his title. He'd had lovers, obviously. They were always vetted to within an inch of their life and his private secretary, Ulmer, damned near applied the condoms to Magnus himself.

Given the absolute dearth of spontaneity and the growing pressure to find a "suitable" partner and produce an heir, Magnus mostly eschewed sex—which probably contributed to his terrible disposition.

He'd grown numb to all of it.

Tonight, however, he'd felt something besides the frustration of living in a cage. Sure, it had been lust, but it was overwhelming lust. The sight of that woman had shaken him awake, spurring him with fierce need. When they danced, her voice and scent and grace had piqued his appetite. Not just for sex, although in his mind her legs had already been around his waist. No, he'd wanted *her*. It wasn't rational or even civilized, but he didn't care. From the moment their eyes had met, he'd made up his mind that she would come to his room.

Then she'd rejected him.

You should talk to your people.

He hated talking to his people. He hated what they said.

Not a good look, sir. Absolutely not.

Magnus had walked out of the gala, loathing these hellish appearances anyway.

He'd bumped into King Felipe of Nazarine on his way to the elevators. They had a friendly acquaintance, both facing a similar challenge of representing a small island nation on the greater world stage. They'd stepped into this breakout room long enough to agree to support each other's position at an upcoming climate conference, then Felipe had escorted his wife, Claudine, to the ballroom.

"I saw a photographer in the mezzanine," Ulmer said, barely looking up from his tablet. "We can avoid him by using the service elevator." He signaled one of the bodyguards to check the catering hall.

At that moment, the door thrust inward.

Magnus caught a glimpse of bronze and blonde, heard a cry of alarm, then his guard shoved the intruder against the wall with far too much force.

"Let her go!" Magnus was across the room before any of the security protocols that had been drilled into him could register. He clasped his bodyguard's shoulder in the bite of his hand and yanked him away from her, damned near throwing him across the room.

"Sir!" That was Ulmer, trying to prevent a scuffle as his bodyguard turned on Magnus in reflex before realizing his employer was the one attacking him.

"She could be armed, sir," the bodyguard said, tugging his jacket straight and keeping a watchful eye on Lexi.

She turned so her back was to the wall, but her shoulders were hunched and her arms were folded upward defensively. She had one hand pressed to her cheek.

"In that dress? Use your eyes!" Magnus took hold of her wrist, trying to draw her hand down so he could examine her cheek.

She shook him off and slid sideways, still darting frightened looks around the room.

"Let me see," Magnus ordered.

He placed himself between her and the rest of the men, trying to remember to be gentle as he crooked his finger under her chin, but he was beside himself with unnatural fury, especially when he saw how red her cheekbone was.

"If this bruises, I'll give you one to match it," he told his bodyguard in Isleifisch. It was a modern version of Old Norse that was more a dialect between Danish and Norwegian, given Isleif's close ties to both countries.

Lexi brushed his hand off her face, still trembling.

"You're safe," Magnus assured her, belatedly switching to English.

She made a choked noise that held such lack of belief,

the hair on the back of his neck rose. Then something caught her attention beyond him.

"There's nothing in there but my phone and room card," she protested crossly. "And that clutch is on loan. Kindly don't destroy it."

Magnus swore and held out his hand to Ulmer, who had turned out the lining of her rhinestone-bedecked handbag.

Ulmer was about to tear the silk open, but replaced the contents and disdainfully handed it to Magnus.

"It's our job to protect you, sir," Ulmer said in English, no hint of apology in his tone. "She's already damaged your reputation. Now she's followed you in here? Why?" He directed that last imperious query to Lexi.

"I wanted privacy to use my phone." She snatched the clutch from Magnus. "You can all go to hell. I have my own threats to deal with." She slid along the wall again, distancing herself as she placed a call.

"All clear, sir." The bodyguard who'd been sent into the service hall came in the far door.

"Even more reason to use a discreet exit," Ulmer muttered and looked expectantly to Magnus.

Magnus ignored the hint to leave. His hackles were still up, his attention fixated on Lexi. He sensed aggression rising off her, but it wasn't directed at them despite how she'd been treated. It was the defensive kind that hunched her shoulders forward.

"Pick up the phone, you— Oh!" She halted as she arrived at the corner and kept her face to the wall. Her voice seethed through her clenched teeth. "How does Carmichael know where I am? Because he's *here*. In

Paris. At my *hotel*. Did Janet post about this trip? Because I told her to wait until I was home. And that *child* you hired as a bodyguard ate a bad shrimp and can't leave the—"

She turned to pace the other way and froze as she saw they were all watching and listening. The flags of color across her cheekbones deepened to crimson. Her mouth tightened.

"Call me back." She ended the call and let her arm fall to her side. Her throat flexed as she swallowed, but she kept her chin up. "Which one of you is in charge?" she asked loftily.

"Ha!" Magnus barked. "Who the hell do you think?"

Her spine stiffened a fraction more. "If you needed a bodyguard right now, immediately, who would you call?"

"Money is no object?"

"It's definitely an object, but so long as I get my money's worth, I'll pay whatever is necessary." She was pretending to take all of this in stride, but he heard the quaver of real fear underpinning her words.

It was disturbing, further abrading his protective instincts.

Magnus touched his smartwatch, sliding his fingertip to place a call.

"Your Royal Highness," a pleasant female voice answered. "How may I assist you?"

"I need someone in Paris as soon as possible, Kiran."

"Can you wait one moment, please?" She put him on hold long enough for Ulmer to mutter a dismay-laden, "Sir."

Magnus understood his private secretary's concern. Magnus was involving the very security firm that trained his own men, but they *were* the best. And they hadn't become the best by allowing themselves to be compromised by actresses with soiled reputations. Involving them would allow Magnus to run a dossier on Lexi and learn very quickly if she posed any real threat to him.

"Sir?" Kiran's voice returned. "My brother, Vijay, is on his way to Paris as we speak. He said he will join you first thing in the morning. If your team forwards more information, he should have everything you require in place by then. Will that suffice?"

"Thank you, Kiran. Lexi Alexander has a stalker, last name Carmichael." He glanced at Lexi.

"Aaron," she provided. "There's ample coverage of it online. I have a restraining order against him."

"Did you get all that? He's here in our hotel," Magnus added.

"I'll make hotel security aware of that and have them forward tapes for any legal action that may arise. Shall I ask them to provide a guard for Ms. Alexander?"

"No," Magnus decided with a leap of dark satisfaction. "She'll be safe with me until Vijay arrives."

Magnus ended the call, then waved Lexi toward the door to the service hall, where one of his bodyguards was still stationed.

She hesitated, but when she thought of walking out to the mezzanine and around to the elevators, toward Carmichael, her blood congealed.

Forcing a swallow past her dry throat, she complied. She ought to protest that she only needed an escort to her own room, but the fact was, she really needed a moment of feeling safe so she could compose herself and think this through.

Not that her brain managed anything except sparking awareness, crammed into an elevator with the prince and three other men. She pressed into the back to make room. Magnus joined her there, facing her, while the rest of the men entered and faced front.

Disapproval was wafting like musky cologne from the white-haired man who'd gone through her handbag. He didn't like her *at all*.

Prince Magnus didn't seem to care. He touched beneath her chin again, angling her face slightly before he caressed her still-tender cheek with the pad of his thumb.

"It's fading."

She touched where the knock had happened, probing, but also using it as an excuse to brush away his touch because it was far too disturbing, sending trickles of sensual awareness into her throat and down to her chest.

"Why are you helping me?" she asked.

"You know why."

A learned cynicism had her wondering if he expected sex in exchange for his help, but she wasn't sure she minded if he did. Which was a troubling thought.

The elevator stopped and opened, allowing fresh oxygen to rush in.

They had arrived in a laundry room where a guard waited. He nodded a confirmation that seemed to reassure everyone.

Magnus took her hand, sending a zing of electricity up her arm and into her torso. He led her through a kitchen where two staff stopped to nod as they went by.

"Are you hungry?" he asked as they moved through a dining area into a luxurious lounge decorated in shades of gray and ivory with accents of sapphire blue. The drapes were closed and several table lamps glowed.

"No. Thank you." She wriggled her hand free of his, then closed it into a fist, holding on to the sensation of his fingers woven between her own.

His bodyguards dispersed in all directions, checking behind doors and stepping onto the terrace, then checking beyond the door to the hall.

"Are *you* in danger?" she was compelled to ask. "You seem to have a lot of protection."

"An abundance of caution. The previous king—my father —" his lip curled with irony "—was assassinated."

"I'm so sorry. That must have been horrible for you."

"It happened years ago. I never met him." He shrugged off his tuxedo jacket and removed his sash, handing them to that circumspect fellow who was still giving off vibes of hostility and suspicion. "Sit. I'll save you the trouble of looking me up."

Magnus hitched his tuxedo trousers and lowered into an armchair that faced the sofa, instantly turning the chair into a throne with the simple act of lounging his magnificent body upon it. He pulled his bow tie free and discarded it on the side table, then released the button at his throat, shoulders relaxing.

She lowered into the corner of the sofa, sparing a moment for how surreal this was, sitting to converse with a prince. The force of his undivided attention was like a spotlight, hot and blinding.

"Isleif was on the brink of financial collapse and King Einer was living high. I mean that literally as well as figuratively. He was a fan of party drugs and places where they're offered in abundance. He had built a network within the government that was helping him cut inside deals for offshore drilling. In exchange for greasing those wheels, he was given anything he wanted. I'm not telling you anything that isn't in the six-part documentary series."

"He sounds…" She cleared her throat. "Larger than life."

"*Corrupt* is the word most use. It's a wonder he only had the one illegitimate child."

"You?" She widened her eyes.

"Yes. And believe me, I've looked for more. So has Queen Katla, his legitimate heir. She took the throne when he died, but she has never been able to conceive. There had long been rumors in the palace that the king had fathered a child with a commoner, after he lost his son, Katla's older brother. She found me and I was brought to the palace as her successor."

"That sounds like a fairy tale."

"Written by the Brothers Grimm, perhaps."

The grumpy assistant returned. He carried an ice bucket and two wineglasses. He showed Magnus the label on the bottle and Magnus nodded.

"No wine for me, thank you. I don't drink alcohol," Lexi said.

"What would you prefer?" Magnus asked.

"Soda with lime?"

He held up two fingers and the other man disappeared with the wine.

"I don't mind if you drink," she said. "My teetotaling is for PR purposes."

His brows lifted in a command for her to elaborate.

Since she was rarely given a chance to tell her side of things, she did.

"When I was sixteen, one of my brother's friends put drugs in my bag. It was hard stuff that I never would have touched. My father managed to keep me from being charged, but I did a stint in rehab, then a year of community service."

In some ways, the counseling had been a blessing. She probably would be a drug addict by now without that perspective, given all she'd been through. At the time, however, her counselor had feared she was in denial, lying about not having a drug issue.

"I live sober now," she added. "It's simpler."

Her phone burbled in her clutch, but she ignored it.

"Probably my brother calling me back," she said when the Prince's gaze dropped to the noise. "Half brother," she clarified. "He runs the entertainment agency that manages me." The agency her career had built, if she wanted to be petty about it, which she definitely did. "Our father was an entertainment lawyer. Mom worked in hair and makeup before I was born. They had an affair, but he was already married. I was born on the wrong side of the blanket, too."

A choked noise came out of Ulmer as he set a soda with lime on the table beside her.

Magnus gave the man a laconic blink. "You have an opinion you wish to share?"

"You know my opinion, sir."

"I do. Pack it with your things from your room."

"You're not firing him!" Lexi blurted. "I get way worse from trolls online. And I know what the press says about me. I don't blame him for wanting to keep you out of that blast radius."

"If only I could fire him," Magnus said with pained tolerance. "Ulmer serves at the pleasure of the queen. Her goal is that I experience no pleasure at all. I'm actually doing him a favor, giving him the means to report truthfully that he made every effort to offer you a bed that wasn't mine, including providing his own."

"I—" Her throat tightened, cutting off her voice while heat suffused her chest. He was taking a lot for granted! Wasn't he?

Maybe not. She kept imagining how it would feel to straddle him in that wide chair while she finished unbuttoning his shirt.

He held her gaze in a way that suggested he knew exactly what she was thinking. And wanted that, too.

The heat under her skin sizzled into her cheeks and streaked downward into the pit of her belly.

"The hotel is full. Ulmer will need to stay in your room. Give him your key. Unless you have something to hide?" Prince Magnus was like a cat, she realized with a leap of her pulse. He appeared lazy and bored, then surprised with a lightning move that trapped his prey in his sharp claws.

"Only a racy historical romance on the night table. Don't lose my place in it," she said as she opened her clutch.

"Send back something for her to wear in the morning," Magnus instructed.

Lexi thought about insisting on going back to her room. She could ask hotel security to check it, but she knew from experience they were no more qualified than Nishan. She would lie awake all night, fretting they had missed something, terrified by every footfall outside her door, waiting for Carmichael or someone else to break in.

"Will you have one of the men look for cameras, please?" she asked as she offered her key. "That's what Carmichael did the last time he got into my hotel room." She shuddered remembering all the snippets of film that had been shown in court.

Ulmer plucked the card from her with a *tsk*.

"I don't want to need protection," she said shakily, using anger to cover the way she was inwardly cringing with shame. She knew exactly how badly she had already tarnished the prince's reputation. Judging from what he'd said of his father, he couldn't afford any smudges.

"I'll see that you have something comfortable to sleep in, too," Ulmer said stiffly.

"Are you suggesting my bed isn't comfortable?" Magnus taunted at the man's back.

Ulmer sniffed and walked away.

"Please don't make this worse for me," Lexi pleaded. "If you needle him, he's liable to plant something incriminating in my room as retaliation."

"He won't. That could blow back on me. Besides, he prefers to tattle so I can be called on the carpet for a lecture from my sister. It's very tiresome. Let's talk about something else."

"Such as?"

"Tell me why your reputation is so far in the gutter."

"Your people haven't told you?"

"They told me you were involved in a lawsuit. That you are a lightning rod for sensationalism. That you encourage it."

"That last part is not true." She sat back and exhaled, wishing there was somewhere far enough she could retreat to. A remote jungle in Indonesia, perhaps? "I've always tried very hard to be professional and a decent role model to the younger generation."

"You've been acting from a young age, Ulmer said."

"I was famous before I knew what acting was. I was a cute baby so Mom put me in commercials for diapers and whatnot. She didn't need the money. Dad paid her support. He paid her to stay in Scottsdale, let's be real. But I had a temperament for it."

"Acting?"

"Being on set and doing as I was told, yes. I'm patient. A bit of a pleaser. I was then, anyway. I was cast in a soap opera and that led to Paisley Pockets."

His brows went up again.

"A girl who shrinks and travels in pockets. That went for six years and it was very wholesome. Then I did some coming-of-age movies and campy comedies and had just landed a part in a superhero movie when the drugs were found. That was my first scandal and a huge setback career-wise. I tried to drop acting, actually, and went back to college, but notoriety followed me. Frat houses would claim I was at their party and it would turn into a riot when fans showed up and I wasn't there. The dean asked me to leave. My father had just died and Hadley took over the agency. I needed to support myself so I let him talk me into doing a reality show that was bikini-based. The money was great, but it got me a fan base I *really* wish I could undo."

"Like the stalker?"

She nodded jerkily. "Carmichael got off on a technicality. I could have appealed, but I had already lost three years of my life to him. And the cost." She rolled her eyes. "There was no upside to staying in that fight. Half the time the press framed it as a stunt I had pulled because I was an attention whore." Tightness invaded her chest. If only people knew how badly she would love to disappear into obscurity. "From a producer's viewpoint, I was too expensive to hire because I need on-set protection. My image was blonde bimbo from the reality series so no one was considering me for serious roles. I couldn't get work, but I needed security."

"From Carmichael? Or are there others?"

"From everyone." She lifted helpless hands. "Most of my fans are perfectly rational and nice, but the volume is challenging. I need walls and gates. Long story short, I became the face of a cosmetic brand that paid for all of that until they switched out some ingredients

DANI COLLINS   35

due to supply chain issues. It was something the FDA hadn't approved. It reacted with other products and people started getting chemical burns."

He swore under his breath.

"It was very bad," she agreed, nauseated every time she thought of it. "I did everything I could to make it right. I took responsibility for promoting it and paid a huge fine. I sold a bunch of my assets to pay the legal fees because people wanted to sue *me*, even though I had nothing to do with creating the actual product. Anyway, I'm not allowed to put my name behind anything anymore, not that anyone wants it. That's another drawback to hiring me. These days, every film has merchandising licenses attached to it. No one wants me to be the next action figure sold to children. I've made a million apologies and I've donated to every organization I can find, but the bottom-feeding gossip sites still frame me as a monster who doesn't care who she harms so long as she gets ahead."

"Tonight was another photo op? Is that why you danced with me?" His tone held a lash of cynicism.

"That's why I stopped dancing with you," she corrected frostily, but her insides shriveled. "I don't want to be performative about giving to charity. I know how icky that is." She hated that she was reduced to this. "But if my mistakes are going to be made into headlines, I might as well have some good press to balance it. Mostly I came here to meet a director who was supposed to attend. Bernadette Garnier." She rubbed her eyebrow. "I have a project I genuinely think she would find interesting. One that could help me stage a comeback or at least keep the lights on a little longer. She wasn't there, though."

He sat in a comfortable slouch as he regarded her, so casually sexy it was difficult to look at him without more fantasies exploding in her head.

He couldn't want her now, though. Not after she'd laid bare all her flaws and drawbacks. He ought to ask her to leave.

Ulmer stalked back into the room. He held a small valise and paused behind Magnus to send her a hard glare over the prince's shoulder.

She held her breath, awaiting banishment.

"I'll text if I need anything," Magnus said without so much as turning his head.

Ulmer's mouth tightened. Seconds later, the door closed firmly behind him.

"He's not wrong," she pointed out, still wobbly on the inside. "I'm accepting your help because I don't have many friends left. I had to come all the way to Europe for a *chance* at work. You don't want to be associated with me."

"True."

The single word was an arrow straight into her chest, stopping her heart and lungs before radiating a sharp pain through her entire being.

He rose in a graceful move that was so abrupt it took her heart on a fresh dip and roll, and offered his hand. "I'll show you to your room."

CHAPTER THREE

HER FINGERS HAD gone cold. She noticed because his hand was hot. His firm clasp seemed to envelop her entire being as he drew her to stand. She felt lifted off the floor, as though she floated behind him as he led her down the hall.

To *her* room.

He paused in the hall where an open door looked into an empty bedroom.

"Use it if you want to. I'll wake you in the morning when Vijay arrives."

She started to walk through, kind of in a daze, but halted belatedly as his words hit her ears. Her equilibrium teetered.

"If I want to?"

Oh, don't, she warned herself. This man was dangerous. Maybe not violent, but he possessed the sort of power that could destroy what was left of her free will and peace of mind.

"I want this night with you, Lexi. I want *you*." His voice was quiet, yet it reverberated enough to make her cells quiver. "You want me, too."

A painful sense of exposure made her feel naked and

obvious. She tried to reassemble her inner defenses, but it was too late. She already knew he'd breached them. So did he.

"But this is not a quid pro quo." The sea of his eyes roiled with the same frustrated conflict she'd seen on the dance floor. He was exerting supreme control over himself, but it took effort for him to leash his most barbaric instincts—which he had in abundance.

Recognizing that atavistic side of him should have terrified her. On some distant plane of consciousness, it did. Another part responded to that wolfish power that wanted to run her to ground, mostly because she already knew he didn't want to kill her. He wanted to *mate*.

It was such a wild, instinctual knowledge, she felt drunk on it. Petrified, yet excited.

"If I go in here, you won't follow me?" She set her hands behind her against the doorjamb, telling herself to step inside and close the door.

Make the smart choice, Lexi.

"I will not. This is your decision."

He braced his hand above her head, as though grasping at the only thing that would keep him from tipping into the room. He stepped close enough she had to tilt her chin up to hold his gaze. Her heart was going a mile a minute.

"Sleep alone or come to my room where you won't get much sleep at all," he clarified thickly.

Raw electricity pulsed through her torso, out to her limbs.

He wasn't touching her, but she felt compressed by his wide presence. Squeezed into making a decision.

Move into the bedroom or step into the hall. Reject him or abandon herself.

"Are you trying to force me to make the decision for both of us? So you can say I seduced you?"

"You seduced me the moment you looked at me."

Same. She swallowed.

"The whole world already saw us together. Things will be said regardless." His gaze traveled all over her face, as though memorizing its contours. "Go inside and close the door. It's the best thing for both of us. I'll only hate you a little for it," he added with a sardonic curl of his lip.

A tiny whimper throbbed in her throat. Being hated didn't bother her. Or, rather, she'd grown numb to it. And he was joking. He wasn't trying to manipulate her. She didn't feel a need to appease him and *make* him like her. No, this yearning went deeper than that. She kept thinking of him saying she'd seen the man in him.

She had the sense he saw the woman in her. He wasn't staring at her chest. He was looking into her eyes. He wasn't sneering at her sordid history. He had asked her to tell him about it and wanted her in spite of it. She wanted what he was really offering her: acceptance.

"I'll hate myself either way," she acknowledged. "What's one more night?"

A growling noise resounded from his chest. Disapproval? Agreement?

He leaned closer. His free hand cupped her throat above the collar of silk, so she became ultra-aware of her quickened pulse as it thumped against his palm. Her breath stuttered.

He nuzzled the corner of her mouth with restless lips, sharpening the yearning within her to a razor's edge. Her hands were trapped in the small of her back as he used his weight to press her into the doorjamb. The wool of his trousers abraded the silk of her gown, shifting the slit open so she felt the coarse fabric against her inner thigh.

She tried to catch her breath, but her breasts were crushed by his chest. A small, helpless sigh escaped her, parting her lips. Her mouth wanted to find his. He was toying with her, though. Touching soft, soft kisses to her chin and the indent of her upper lip and beneath the pout of her lower one.

Her lips stung with anticipation as he teased her. When she couldn't stand it any longer, she flicked out her tongue, striking against the smooth flesh of his bottom lip.

With a gruff noise, he angled his mouth across hers, smothering her small cry of surprise as he swept her into a stark, untamed place. Colors shot behind her closed eyelids.

In an instant, she was both trapped and utterly free. Soaring. There was a vague discomfort at the back of her head where it was pressed to uneven wood, but she was far more conscious of the hardness against her abdomen, his arousal unmistakable despite the layers of their clothes.

"This is what you want?" His mouth roamed across her cheek and his teeth lightly clamped near the stud in her ear. Every hair on her body stood up.

She shouldn't want this. Of the many things she wanted,

above all she wanted to feel safe. This man was not safe. He wouldn't hurt her. She was as sure about that as she could be, but he wasn't promising more than a few hours of pleasure. Her instincts for self-preservation, honed to a fine point by a lifetime of dealing with users and syco-phants, were utterly failing her where he was concerned. She could feel herself succumbing to him because she was unwilling to fight herself.

One night, she kept repeating to herself. One night of pleasure. Of forgetting. She was entitled, wasn't she?

It wouldn't be enough. She already knew that. She wanted to know him more than physically. She wanted to know him intimately—even though she had the sense he would remain an enigma his whole life, never allow-ing anyone to really know him.

Everything about their coming together was tragically ill-advised, but her desire to be in his orbit, to feel his touch and hold his attention and *be* his for even a very short while, was too tempting to resist.

With a small shudder, she let go of doubt and worry about repercussions and surrendered to the inevitable. "Yes."

He lifted his head and stepped back. "Go to my room, then."

Her stomach was full of butterflies that soared into her chest. She led him to the end of the hall on shaking legs, hyperaware of his heavy steps behind her.

His room was extravagantly beautiful. The ceiling gleamed with copper tiles that glowed like a sunset above the wide, turned-down bed. Frothy sheers over solid drapes covered the tall windows. A thickly loomed area rug cushioned her step, making the click of the door lock seem overly loud.

She was staring at the bed, mouth dry, when he came up behind her. He swept her hair to the front of her shoulder. The snug collar of her gown eased as he released its two buttons.

"I don't...do this," she said, voice unsteady.

He paused in unhooking the clasp above the zip near her tailbone. "Have one-night stands? Or have sex? You're not a virgin."

"I don't have casual sex." She rarely had sex. Her attempts at relationships always fizzled. Too many men were trophy hunters or manipulators, but that was why Magnus appealed to her so much. He didn't want anything from her but *her*.

"Neither do I." His fingertips trailed absently along her spine, down and up and down again. "But this doesn't feel casual."

He was right. It felt profound.

He released the hook and slid the short zipper.

"This gown is on loan. I need to be careful with it," she said as she caught the front.

He helped her step out of it, then gave it a light shake before draping it across the bench at the end of the bed. He turned to look at her as he popped his cuffs and opened the buttons on his shirt.

"It's not very sexy." She had stood before cameras often enough in minimal clothing that she shouldn't have been so self-conscious in her underwear. Heck, the black halter bra and high-cut, tummy-control panties were more modest than most bikinis she wore.

Nevertheless, as his attention wandered leisurely over her, she shifted on her heels.

"I'm not mad at it." He opened his fly and dragged his shirt out, baring most of his torso as he padded toward her. "These straps are kind of hot." He traced from where they met behind her neck down to the corset-like under-band beneath her breasts. His fingers splayed against the cups, plumping her breasts into the deep cut of the cleavage.

She didn't know where to put her hands and let them settle nervously on his sleeves.

He was really...everything. Powerful. Broad and muscular and emanating a spicy masculine scent that she knew she would remember for the rest of her life.

She didn't want to look and think and wonder where to put her hands, though. She wanted the blind passion that made her *feel*. She stepped forward, gaze on his mouth, and tilted hers up in invitation.

His mouth came down in a passionate crush, sweeping her back into that place where she didn't think about how she looked or who she was or what the consequence of this might be. She gave herself over to him, not realizing he was moving her with the same fluid confidence he'd used on the dance floor until the cool wall met her shoulder blades.

"What...um...?" She tried to catch her breath, but couldn't. Not when she was looking into raw lust glowing deep within his eyes.

He began to roll her underwear down her hips. He crouched to set a small kiss on the skin he exposed above her navel, then below it. Her mind blanked as his tender assault continued. Another kiss branded the point of her hip. He sent a soft "Hah" against her bared folds, stirring the fine hairs, making her flesh throb with anticipation.

His lips nuzzled the crease at the top of her thigh as he helped her step out of her panties.

"Do you know what high ceilings are good for?" he asked as he blew gently against her folds again.

She could hardly make sense of his words. She shook her head, thinking, *I can't breathe.*

In a formidable move, he swept his arms under her thighs, rising at the same time.

A startled scream escaped her. She scrambled for purchase against the wall, knocking a painting askew and catching a fistful of his bound hair.

"You're safe, goddess." His breath was between her legs, her thighs braced on his shoulders. His wide hands splayed under her butt supported her. "I'm here to worship. I won't let you fall."

Her choke of disbelief turned to a fresh cry of surprise when he set his teeth in playful warning against the sensitive skin of her inner thigh.

Her legs quivered in reaction, trying to close, but it was too late. He buried his mouth against her nether lips and scored her with the wet lash of his tongue.

She was at his mercy, completely unable to get away. It was raw intimacy and exquisite sensations.

He wanted to annihilate her, she thought wildly. Nothing would be the same after this. Nothing.

But as hot spears of pleasure emanated upward and outward, filling her with joyous light, she didn't care. She wanted him to wreck her. She pushed the back of her head against the wall and worked her hands with sensual agitation into his hair, not bothering to stifle her moans of pleasure. The bodyguards in the hall outside the suite could probably hear her and she didn't care.

No one had ever done this to her. *For* her. She *felt* worshipped. She felt like a goddess. Pure. Powerful. Deserving.

She arched her back, angled her hips and guided his head, gasping, "There. Please."

He found the perfect rhythm with his tongue, lavishing her with intensely sweet, generous attention. It was so good, it was almost painful, yet she begged him, "More. Don't stop." Waves of heat built in her core. Her stomach knotted with tension. Her legs stiffened and her toes pointed. She bit her lip, trying to reach the pinnacle. "Please, Magnus. Please."

Climax arrived with the blinding force of a lightning strike. While she shuddered and jolted in paroxysms of pleasure, her moans of ecstasy bounced off the high ceiling and echoed around the room.

Magnus was shaking with exertion when Lexi's body slumped into weighty gratification.

He let her slide down until he could catch her in the cradle of his arms. He was so acutely aroused he wanted to throw her on the bed and fling himself on top of her, driving into her like an animal.

"I need a condom," he reminded himself, and went into the bathroom to get them from his case. He splashed cold water onto his face while he was there, trying to regain some semblance of control.

She was magnificent. His perfect match. The fact he only had one night with her infuriated him. A lengthy affair with her was one more thing he couldn't have and he wanted to bellow his rage at the world for it.

He dried his beard and walked back into the bedroom to find her waiting in his bed, sitting against the pillows with a sheet pulled up to cover her breasts. The black straps of her bra were gone. Her shoes were on the floor beside the monogrammed slippers he never used.

All the bitter acrimony within him hardened into a diamond that glittered and sent out shards of hunger and anticipation and lust. *One night.* He would make the most of it.

He removed a condom from the box and left the box on the night table, then clutched the packet in his teeth while he pulled the cord from his hair. The pewter wolf's head landed next to the box. He gave his hair a loose comb with his fingers, shaking it out.

She watched him, keeping the edge of her lip in her teeth as he stripped off the rest of his clothes. By the time he was naked, her eyes had widened with wariness.

"Still with me, goddess?" he asked gruffly. The beast in him snarled, unwilling to be denied.

"Nervous," she said in a small voice.

"Why?" He applied the condom and threw back the covers, exposing her very enticing form.

She let out a squeak of surprise and wriggled sideways, leaving ample room on the mattress for him to settle beside her.

He braced on his elbow, appreciating the endless expanse of pale skin that held a hint of gold. Her full, up-tilted breasts had beige nipples pebbled with arousal, making his mouth water. Then there was the shadowy valley between her shyly clamped thighs, calling to him.

"Did I not demonstrate that I'm an extremely considerate lover?" He traced a light caress from her ankle to her knee, then up her thigh to her hip.

Her breasts quivered as she took a shaken breath.

"I plan to give you so many orgasms, you won't have the strength to say, *Thank you, Magnus.*"

The noise she made was a catch between a sob and a laugh. "I want to call you arrogant, but I'm afraid you're only telling the truth."

"Let's find out, shall we?" He scooped his arm around her hips, dragging her close enough he could open his mouth on one of the very pretty nipples that were tempting him so irresistibly.

As he rolled the firm berry against his tongue, she moaned and ran her hands into his hair.

"I didn't know I had a kink for men with long hair," she confided in a husky voice. "But I like how it feels."

"Don't talk about other men." He was not so hypocritical he thought women shouldn't take lovers, but he didn't want to think about her with anyone but him.

He rose enough to press her onto her back and swept his mouth to her other nipple, taking his time as he laved and sucked, enjoying the way she slid her fingers through his hair as he did.

When he couldn't wait any longer, he rose to kiss her, needing the feel of her lips opening against his own. Needing the brush of her tongue when he invaded.

And she was welcoming here, too. He strayed his

hand between her thighs and found her soft and plump and slick. He wanted to taste her again. He wanted to live his life with the right to explore her like this, easing his touch into silken heat, feeling her muscles clamp snugly around his exploring finger while her breath hitched.

Her eyes were hazed with carnal need. He looked from that exquisite sight to the roll of her hips as she lifted to meet the slow thrust of his hand.

"Show me how you like to be touched." He needed to learn *exactly* how to please her, right now, because he didn't have a lifetime to learn it.

He didn't have a lifetime to practice, either.

"Magnus, please." She swept her hands across his shoulders, then wriggled her hand between them, closing her hand around his girth. "I want to feel this. *You.*"

He could have lost himself right there, from only her soft grip and erotic words. It killed him to give up touching her, but he shifted to settle between her thighs, pushing them wide with his knees to make room for his hips.

"I'm a strong man, Lexi." He was built tall and wide and burned off a lot of sexual frustration in the weight room. "I *really* want you." More than he'd ever wanted anyone. Ever. But he wasn't going to dwell on how disconcerting that was. Not when he was at heaven's gate. "Stop me if I get too rough."

"You won't."

She didn't know, though. She didn't know how badly he wanted to make her his.

Leaning his weight on one elbow, he guided himself

to her entrance and probed. Everything in him wanted to thrust to his root, but her nails bit into his upper arm.

He froze and looked at where she was pinching his biceps.

"Sorry." She rubbed the spot. "I really want this to be good for you."

"Look where I am." He nibbled the edge of her jaw. "This is very good."

He flared his nostrils to take in oxygen, trying to keep a few brain cells working as her heat closed around his tip, threatening to burn him alive. He let his weight do the work, slowly settling his pelvis onto hers as he forged his way into a sensation that dimmed his vision.

As he arrived deep inside her, his back flexed with pleasure.

"Oh," she breathed shakily, as though discovering something new. Then she bent her leg to sweep one foot against the back of his calf.

The movement drew him a fraction deeper into paradise. Her hands stroked his ribs and caressed his back and found his buttocks. She tilted back her head and made a noise of luxury.

The outside world disintegrated. All that existed was her and this: the drag and thrust of lovemaking and the profound pleasure it gave them both.

Lexi woke cotton-headed. She was in a dark room. The tangled weight of Magnus's limbs pinned her to the mattress.

He was entitled to his arrogance, was her first lazy

thought. He had delivered a string of orgasms that had nearly broken her in half.

"Stay," he grumbled when she tried to pull away.

"Nature calls." She dragged herself to the bathroom and used the toilet, then slipped on the hotel robe while she washed off her makeup.

Magnus came in, casually naked and burnished bronze by the muted night-light. He wordlessly handed her a toothbrush from a drawer, still in its packet. Then he closed himself into the toilet stall, emerging a moment later to brush his own teeth.

"Do you mind?" She picked up his hairbrush.

"Help yourself."

Her hair was nothing but knots, given the styling products she'd used earlier, then the sweaty lovemaking while he had tumbled her this way and that on the bed. He had seemed determined to wring every last sensation from every position he could dream up, all while making her his in the most indelible ways.

It had worked. She had thought she had a low libido, never discovering true passion no matter how many toads she kissed.

Tonight she'd kissed a prince, she thought with amusement.

She watched him cup his hand under the running faucet to rinse his mouth. He straightened and used a hand towel to dry his beard, stilling when he noticed her watching.

"What are we thinking, pretty bird?"

"That this feels like a dream."

His rumbled noise might have been agreement. He

took the hairbrush from her and moved behind her, running it smoothly through the length since she'd already done most of the work.

People fussed with her hair all the time, but this felt different. His hand petted behind every stroke, as though he took as much pleasure in this act as she did. He was a prince, for heaven's sake. What was he doing, playing attentive lady's maid?

A scald of heat arrived behind her eyes that didn't make any sense. Or rather, she didn't want to pick apart why she felt so emotive. In this moment, she felt cared for, truly cared for, even though this was only sex. Once morning arrived, they would never see each other again.

"I don't want to wake up." She didn't realize she said it aloud until his gaze met hers in the mirror.

The hairbrush landed next to the sink and his arms came around her, drawing her backward into him. One hand dived behind her lapel to cup her breast. Her nipple tightened to a point against his palm. His other hand burrowed below the tied belt, finding the quivering jump of her stomach.

"I don't want to sleep," he said in a graveled voice. He nuzzled against her hair, seeking her ear. "Are you sore? Or—? Mmm…" A satisfied noise left him as he traced into her folds and found her slick enough to bloom against his touch.

She was very tender, but his touch was lazy and gentle. Even so, she was so sensitized, the friction was almost too intense to bear.

She covered his hand, stilling his touch, but felt his

erection against her bottom, through the thick velour of the robe.

"I'll be so careful, Lexi," he whispered against her ear, tongue dabbling into the whorls, teeth teasing the rim. "Do you really want me to stop?"

"No," she admitted, closing her eyes against the watchful glitter of his gaze.

His heavy hand lifted beneath the weight of hers. His touch was barely there, but the knot of nerves at the top of her sex was so swollen, the barest roll of his fingertip had her turning her face into his shoulder. A groan of helpless desire escaped her throat.

"Tell me no one else gives you this," he commanded.

"No one," she gasped, arching her bruised nipple into his palming hand. Climax danced as elusively as his caress between her thighs.

"You make me feel like a god." He pressed his wide, claiming hand over her mound.

Her hips instinctively pushed into that firm hold and she broke, awash in sensations that melted her bones, but that was okay. His strong arms kept her from falling.

He woke her once more in the night, rolling away long enough to put on a condom, then stayed spooned behind her while they spent a long time simply enjoying the sensation of being joined, caressing and kissing what skin they could reach, sighing with bliss into the dark.

When orgasm arrived, it came in long, rolling pulses that took Lexi out to sea like a tide. She drifted to sleep still rocked by the waves of pleasure.

Magnus must have fallen asleep, too. She had a vague

memory of waking with a start when he drew a breath and hardened inside her.

His arms tightened around her and he said something in his language before he asked, "Are you asleep?"

She made a noise between dismay and reassurance, wincing slightly at the sensation as he withdrew, but she didn't want to leave this liminal state between dream and waking.

He rolled away, then came back to envelop her and kiss her shoulder. They both sighed and slid back into dreamland.

CHAPTER FOUR

IF IT WERE up to Magnus, he would have kept Lexi in his bed indefinitely, but it was never up to him.

Resentment was a wasted emotion, though. He had wallowed in buckets of it through those early years of learning who he was, but it hadn't retrieved any of what he'd lost. The man he had believed was his father was still firmly gone, turning his back in a way that still tightened Magnus's chest.

His siblings hadn't known whose side to take and Magnus had been needed here so there'd been a wedge there, too. His brother and sister were strangers to him now. There was nothing left of their childhood camaraderie. He'd even lost his mother, to some extent. While he had come to understand and accept her reasons for hiding his paternity, he'd lost a measure of trust in her that could never be regained.

But sacrifice to the crown was not just expected or desired. It was required. Becoming a king meant he couldn't indulge the man within him.

Or keep the woman who had given that man more pleasure than he could stand.

Steeling himself against the ire and bitterness over

what felt like yet another theft from his life, he finished dressing and went back into the shadowy bedroom where he sat on the edge of the bed.

Lexi's neck was warm and soft. Her shift into wakefulness stirred his desire to crawl back into those sheets and lose himself again, but he made himself pull his hand away before she had finished fluttering her eyelids.

She tried to get her bearings by glancing at the clock and the place where daylight was coming through the cracks in the drapes.

"I let you sleep as long as I could. Ulmer is running a bath in the guest room. Your clothes are there. Vijay will be here shortly."

He leaned to snap on a lamp, flooding the room with more harsh reality that made her wince. He made himself stand and lift the robe off the foot of the bed, holding it ready for her, catching a flash of stunned hurt on her expression before she schooled it.

He didn't allow it to move him. This was his life. There was no changing it.

"Ulmer has your gown. He'll make arrangements for its return."

She said a small "Thank you" before she started to sit up. A strangled groan left her.

"That's why the bath," he said drily. He had felt as though he'd been hit by a truck when he rose. There was a certain euphoria in the ache of his sore muscles, though. He liked it.

With another muted whimper, she rose to thread her arms into the robe, hurrying to close it and fumbling with the belt, head ducked.

It was a bit late for shyness or embarrassment. It wasn't shame, was it? That thought bothered him, but she hurried out and he could hear Vijay arriving so he went to the lounge.

Vijay Sahir was second in command at TecSec, a world-renowned private security firm. Vijay always wore a calm demeanor along with an exceptionally nice suit. Not flashy, but reassuringly authoritative. His wife and her twin were fashion designers. They knew how to make an impression and Vijay always made a quiet yet powerful one.

After a brief handshake, he accepted a coffee and told Magnus he had forwarded a report on Lexi and the various threats against her. And, because he was very good at his job, the report summarized the threats Lexi posed to Magnus.

While sipping his own coffee, Magnus read through them.

Her reputation was top of the list, obviously. It was sullied enough that their dance would have a knock-on effect to his own, but associating with him gave her social cache she badly needed. Was that why she had invaded the breakout room last night and come up here with him?

Magnus didn't want to believe it, but the state of her finances was listed as a potential threat. She had alluded to financial strain and a need to find work. The report didn't outright accuse her of looking for a bailout or a sugar daddy, but the implication was there.

As for threats against her, Vijay had identified possible malfeasance by the agency that her brother ran, but he couldn't rule out their colluding on those things.

Damn. Given his position, Magnus could not afford to be anything less than suspicious of her. Last night began to seem more calculated on Lexi's part. She was an actress, after all.

Her had already resigned himself to having to distance from her, but now it became imperative.

Lexi didn't linger in the tub of lavender-scented water, even though she was completely disoriented by all that had happened and really needed time alone to put it all in perspective.

She was most especially disturbed by the remoteness that had come over Magnus after their intimate, passionate night. He couldn't have made it more clear that their night was over. She had known it wasn't the start of anything long-lasting, but she hadn't expected him to turn off like a light switch.

His businesslike demeanor had made her feel self-conscious about her nudity and a sense of being *too* naked had her rising abruptly from the water without washing her hair.

She dressed in the dark purple suit with an oyster-colored blouse that Ulmer had brought for her. His attention to detail meant she had everything: underwear, shoes, even a small toiletry bag with her hairbrush and makeup to hide the shadows beneath her eyes.

When she left the bedroom, she looked as professional as she would on a press junket, but she felt horribly exposed as she entered the lounge.

A man of South Asian descent rose from the sofa.

Magnus stayed seated. He set aside a tablet and lifted his incisive gaze to her, making her hyperaware of herself. She had to concentrate on not letting her ankles wobble or her smile falter.

"You must be Vijay." She offered her hand. "Good morning."

"Ms. Alexander. It's a pleasure to meet you. My children have discovered reruns of your show. The theme song is embedded in my ears."

"I didn't write it, but I always feel I owe parents an apology for it." She took a seat on the sofa opposite Vijay. "Do you live here in Paris? I hope I didn't tear you away from vacation."

"My wife's family is here and we have an office here. It's very normal that I have business when we visit. Shall we get to it? I have some concerns."

"Oh?"

Vijay didn't look at Magnus, but she felt the prince's gaze on her. She had the very strong sense she was about to learn something Magnus already knew.

"The X-Calibur Entertainment Agency. Your father started it?"

"Yes, but why is that relevant?" Why was her body suddenly buzzing with adrenaline?

"I like a big picture view. It allows me to see patterns. You have a silent stake in the company. Is that correct?"

"I'm a client, so I don't have anything to do with the day-to-day running. That could raise conflicts of interest." Accusations that she was given opportunities based on nepotism, as opposed to merit.

"But you receive a share of profits."

"I do." She was starting to feel like Swiss cheese, given all the holes that Magnus was drilling into her with his gaze.

"X-Calibur manages all aspects of your career? Contracts, PR, legal."

"All aspects of my life, really. Everything down to the guy who delivers my groceries. My father always had a 'keep it in the family' attitude."

"Which means you trust the agency?"

"Completely." She said it with confidence, but had the strangest sensation that the floor tilted beneath her couch. "Why? Is there a reason I shouldn't?"

Vijay briefly cocked his head, and she felt totally thrown off-balance.

"X-Calibur has a hundred clients," she rushed to say, as though it proved something. "It exists because of me and my early career. They wouldn't do anything to jeopardize my ability to make them money." It was cold-blooded, but it was the way it had always been.

"I think it's how they make that money that deserves a second look," Vijay said in a neutral tone.

Her heart took a dip. "What do you mean?"

"You pay them to protect you, but I don't see an incentive for them to actually do that. Not when bad publicity and court cases generate so much revenue for them."

"The incentive is that I'm a creative asset. I make them money by *acting*."

"Do you?" Magnus asked.

His simple question was a harsh one-two slap, both

of them awful. No, she wasn't getting acting jobs lately, and he didn't have to rub her nose in it, thanks. But as she met his iced-over gaze, she heard the darker side of his question. The suspicion. Was she acting *now*? Had she been acting last night?

"You're accusing me of staging all of this?" She waved at her presence in his suite. "I didn't even know who you were yesterday. *You* asked *me* to dance. You brought me up here. I wish I could get men to do what I want just by thinking about it," she added in a mutter. "I'd rule the damned world."

Magnus only stroked his hand over his beard while he continued to watch her.

Whatever delicate threads of connection had formed between them overnight snapped, leaving her feeling adrift in the cold vacuum of space, but she was used to that. It was happening on more than one level, in real time, as she absorbed that her family was not looking after her best interest, content to line their pockets at her expense.

"Are you suggesting it's no accident that my bodyguard was underqualified and my stalker knew where to find me?" she asked Vijay.

"If it's not deliberate sabotage, it's gross incompetence."

She rose to take a few agitated steps, mind exploding under this new perspective on her relationship with her brother and sister.

There had always been petty jealousies from that quarter. Lexi had been a hot property as a child. The more involved her father was in her life and career, the more rights he had had to the money she generated. His legitimate children had resented her taking his attention and gaining his approval even as her work paid for their vacations and electronics and other frills.

Lexi had always believed that those frills were enough to keep them on her side. They wouldn't shoot down the rocket that was taking them to the moon, would they?

An old suspicion tickled at her. She had always wondered if Hadley had set her up with those drugs. Her father had refused to hear it, but Hadley had been a little too happy that she'd lost that superhero role. Then, after their father died, he had talked her into that reality series, constantly pushing an image of her as a sexpot, spoiling her chances at roles with more substance.

She began to shake with a mix of fury and fear, incensed with herself for being blind to what seemed obvious, now that it was pointed out to her. She was also daunted by the fight ahead of her, but her gut told her she had to cut ties with X-Calibur and Hadley and Janet along with it.

"Firing them will be a nightmare." She was thinking aloud. "They have the machine in place to destroy me before I could pull myself free. I would need resources I don't have."

"Vijay also has a machine." Magnus broke into her thoughts, making her heart lurch. "One that caters to clients with more to lose than an acting career. I'll cover whatever expenses exceed your budget."

Ulmer cleared his throat, registering his disapproval.

It was demoralizing enough that Magnus was learning how badly her family treated her—and was offering to give her *money*. It was even worse that the judgmental Ulmer was witnessing all of it.

She gathered what little dignity she had left and said, "That's not necessary. I'll figure it out."

"I have a vested interested in keeping my name out of it," Magnus stated, turning the knife. To Vijay, he said, "Whatever it costs to tidy this up is fine."

You bastard, Lexi thought, fighting the heat that rose behind her eyes. Last night, he couldn't keep his hands off her. Today he would pay any amount to have his hands washed clean of her.

"Once I sell my share in the agency, I'll have ample funds to pay you back." She would sell her soul to ensure she cleared any debt she incurred with him. "Why don't we take this to my room so we can hammer out an action plan?" she said to Vijay.

Magnus rose as Vijay did.

Did Magnus think he was invited? Hell, no.

"Vijay can keep you updated," she said, channeling the most haughty of daytime soap divas. "To reassure you that none of this will splash back on you. Thank you for your assistance, Your Royal Highness. I feel I'm in better hands already."

Did her comment border on bitchy? Yes. But she was feeling stung and cheapened and *paid for*.

The glint of cynical amusement in Magnus's eye told her the remark landed, which gave her no satisfaction. She only felt obvious in her disgrace.

"Your things have already been returned to your room, Ms. Alexander." Ulmer moved to the door. "Any future communication may go through Mr. Sahir."

It was an ultra-polite *I hope we never hear from you again*.

As she walked out the door, she flickered him a dour look that said, *Same*.

CHAPTER FIVE

"LET'S GET THIS over with," Magnus said as he strode into the queen of Isleif's formal receiving room.

"Do not be so dismissive," Katla said coldly. "No, you may not sit. And you. Out." She waved Ulmer and the palace secretary, Yngvar, from the room.

Ansgar Palace was built behind the original castle, which stood on a bluff overlooking Isleif's main port. This room of relics and modern conveniences had a sunny view past the north tower in the mornings, but today the harbor wore a carpet of mist that obscured all but the highest rigging on the container ships unloading their wares.

"I am thirty-two years old, Your Majesty," Magnus said with pithy, exaggerated patience. "I do not appreciate being treated as though I'm *two*."

"Welcome to the royal family, Magnus. It comes with expectations that you behave like an adult in order to be treated like one. When you fail to do that, you will be scolded. What were you *thinking*?" Her voice was not overloud, but held enough dismay to ring in his ears.

"That I wanted to get laid—which is a very adult occupation." His aim was to offend, but he immediately regretted his crudeness. Vijay might have handed him a bouquet of red flags where Lexi was concerned, but she had been more than a piece of tail.

"Get yourself a wife if that's what you want," Katla said.

"What century is this? I won't marry for sex."

"You'll marry because you must."

"No." Despite the way they locked horns, he didn't hate his half sister. He hated the way he had found out about her. He hated the world she had dragged him into. He hated the power she had over him, not because of her title, but because he liked and respected her. He hated that she held him to a higher standard than he wished to adhere to. He hated that he hated to disappoint her. He hated that she was almost always *right*.

"I can't have children, Magnus. I have tried." Her voice was pitched between the weariness of having to repeat herself and the steely tone she used when her emotions were riled. "It falls to you."

"Why?" he demanded, also weary with this conversation. "You were considering adoption before you found me. Why is that not still an option? You *want* children."

"I'm too busy with the colicky infant I have, aren't I?" She rose in a rustle of her bespoke pantsuit, walking away to hide her expression. "I have continued to hope that I could somehow…" Her voice trailed off, then resounded with heavy fatalism. "They won't let me try another surrogate. My frozen eggs have been deemed unviable."

She was fifty-four and had spent the better part of three decades trying to produce an heir. A twinge of pity had him backing down. Katla wanted children, truly wanted them. Not for the crown, although that was expected, but for herself and her husband, Prince Sorr.

Magnus didn't really understand the impulse. Yes, he had fond memories from his youth, but he mostly remembered a desire to hurry those years. He'd been impatient to grow up so he could pursue his own interests. His younger siblings, with their shorter legs and dependence on his greater maturity, had been an encumbrance who had held him back.

An old spear of guilt went through him at taking them for granted. He would go back to those days in a heartbeat if he could, but he still didn't understand the urge to take responsibility for another human life. Katla already held responsibility for all the lives in a kingdom. Who the hell would want to raise a child with the expectation that they must shoulder the same burden? Given all Magnus had learned about duty to a crown, bringing a child into this role struck him as an act of cruelty.

As though Katla knew what he was thinking, she said, "You of all people should not be advocating I snatch a child from the street and turn them into my heir. No, Magnus, that is your cross to bear."

He knew. He could fight it all he wanted, but it had been drilled into him from the time his DNA had proved he came from the Thorolf bloodline that he would continue that line.

"Could you have chosen anyone more unsuitable with which to dally?" she grumbled.

"Shall I try?"

"I have already made a career of apologizing for one

man's behavior." Katla turned to him, tall and regal and firm. Her expression was dispassionate. "Do not make your inability to keep your libido in check *my* cross to bear."

"It was one night," he said through his teeth. "As far as the world is concerned, we danced *once*." Thanks to Vijay and his concisely worded threats to hotel management, any proof that Magnus had done anything more with the notorious Lexi Alexander was firmly erased, suppressed and filed under "unfounded gossip."

"Ulmer tells me you're paying for her security detail?"

"Why do you employ a man who can't keep his mouth shut?" He turned to face the window. "File it under charitable donations," he added in an ironic drawl.

"You can't support her, Magnus. You had an affair, fine. It's done. But let it be done."

"Paying for her protection is the most expedient way to ensure my own. As long as I'm footing the bill, I'm as much Vijay's client as she is."

That's why Vijay had given him the report that had raised all of Magnus's suspicions around her motives. In his quest to detach himself from her, Magnus had expected every reaction from wheedling to defensive anger. She'd only been insulted. Hurt. And pale with shock over what she'd learned about her family.

"I haven't spent the last two decades restoring peace and prosperity so you can set us back by chasing skirt." Katla's demeanor turned regal. This was no longer a discussion. It was a decree. "People need to see stability and continuity. You must marry, Magnus. Produce children. Show them what the future looks like."

It was not a future he longed for. Why would it inspire anyone else?

"I've asked Ulmer to prepare a list. Introductions will begin in the next few weeks." She rang the bell to dismiss him.

It might as well have been the rattle of a guillotine blade coming down.

Over the next eight weeks, Lexi leaned heavily on the small but mighty team that Vijay had put in place for her. They were astonishingly competent, giving her the fairly simple task of stalling Hadley and any other calls from the agency while they quietly set up a chain of events like dominoes.

Thank goodness they were good at their jobs, because she was a wreck. She blamed her forgetfulness and moments of emotional tearfulness on the upheaval of realizing her family had absolutely no regard for her, but the deeper ache was Magnus.

Which was stupid. She'd spent one night with him, whereas Hadley and Janet were fixtures in her life. There had always been animosity there, though. With Magnus, for at least a few hours, she'd thought there'd been accord. Synchronicity. Something powerful that was—

An illusion, she reminded herself harshly.

Sex. They had had sex. It was good sex, which was nothing to be ashamed of. The shame was in her pining for a man who had wondered after the fact if she had singled him out for her own gain.

She was the one who had been used. Did he really believe she would do that to someone else?

Apparently, he did.

I have a vested interested in keeping my name out of it.

She felt sick, literally nauseous, every time she thought of that horrible morning.

Don't think of it.

Today was a big day. Not only did she finally have a meeting scheduled with Bernadette Garnier, but Lexi's new lawyer would walk into Hadley's office this afternoon and present her brother with the one-two punch of informing him that she was leaving as a client and also wanted to sell her share in the agency. Hadley had the right of first refusal, but she knew for a fact that her leaving the roster would impact the agency's value, especially if bad press followed.

Hadley had a decision to make. Did he want to sign an NDA and settle things quietly? Or cause them both to suffer financially by making it public that she was leaving? She had a very unflattering statement prepared on how poorly he'd treated her. He would want to think twice about starting a PR war.

At this point, Lexi didn't care how much money she came away with, so long as she was free. She hated herself for trusting Hadley as long as she had. It undermined her confidence in herself and her own decisions.

She also hated that she had Magnus to thank for bringing Vijay's shrewd assessment into the picture.

It meant that she couldn't paint Magnus as a heartless villain and absolve herself of responsibility for their night together.

No, she'd been a very willing participant and she was a weak-minded fool for wishing she could have had more time with him.

With a frustrated groan, she left her walk-in closet, startled to find her mother setting up at the dressing table.

"What's wrong?" Rhonda asked.

"Nothing. I didn't realize you were here already." Lexi threw a handful of blouse selections onto the bed.

"Are you nervous?" Her mother waved at the seat. "Is that why you called me to do your makeup instead of using Sharla? You're going to be great, doll. You always land these things."

Not true, but Rhonda had never let Lexi wallow in discouragement. She was a faithful cheerleader, but she had also pushed her daughter too hard from too early an age.

"I hadn't seen you lately," Lexi prevaricated. "This was a good excuse to catch up." And she no longer trusted Sharla, who was yet another technician booked through the agency.

Lexi hadn't told her mother she was leaving X-Calibur. Rhonda still had a lot of ill will against Lexi's father. Lexi had learned a long time ago not to bring up her father's family at all with her mother if she could help it.

"How are things with Wayne?" she asked instead, listening as Rhonda complained about the car her boyfriend had bought her. He was twenty years her senior and had a very nice house in Malibu that her mother had moved into. Her mother had always known how to take care of herself.

"Why are you so pale?" Rhonda asked as she blended the foundation across Lexi's forehead and cheeks.

"I can't even go onto the balcony for sun. There was a drone out there the other day."

"Hmm. Well, I don't want you to look like you're trying too hard. I'm using a light hand. Wear the pink top." She flickered her gaze to the bed. "That will put some color into your face. But if I didn't know better..." She turned Lexi's face in each direction, expression concerned.

"What?" Lexi demanded.

"Nothing." Her mother dug through her case for a different brush. "You said it was only a dance. I believe you. You haven't been seeing anyone else, have you?" She slid a sideways look at Lexi.

"Like a man? I'm not pregnant, Mom!" Lexi didn't have to act shocked. It genuinely hadn't occurred to her. They had used condoms.

"Good. I did my time with a baby on set. I won't go back to it." Her mother worked on her eyes, sweeping contouring strokes and colors over her closed eyelids. "The baby would be a prince or something, wouldn't it? Think of the security you'd need! And custody? You know how ugly things became with your father."

"Mom." She caught her mother's hand. "Please. Trust me. I'm not pregnant." Absolutely not. It couldn't happen. No, no, no.

But even her wildly unpredictable cycle had never gone a full two months without showing up.

A cold sweat took hold in Lexi's lower back as she realized she hadn't had a period since before Paris.

She couldn't be pregnant, though. Magnus had used condoms.

And he really would hate her if that happened.

I have a vested interest...

It took all her control to pretend she wasn't dizzy and clammy while her mother finished her makeup and did her hair.

"Break a leg, baby." Her mother kissed the air near her cheek. "Text me later, tell me how it goes."

"I will." She smiled weakly.

After her mother left, Lexi rose, still feeling light-headed. She called to make a doctor's appointment while she dressed, then walked to her waiting car.

Her mind couldn't seem to grasp a proper thought. The drive through the city happened without her awareness. Suddenly Ola, her favorite bodyguard, was standing on the curb outside the open back door of the SUV.

"All right, Lexi?"

"Pardon? Yes. Just thinking."

Snap out of it, she berated herself.

But what would this mean for her chances for landing *any* role if she was pregnant? At least her shares in the agency provided her a small but predictable income. If—

No. She would worry about a baby if there was one. In this moment, she wasn't pregnant. She absolutely could not be.

She walked through the lobby of Bernadette's hotel

feeling as though she walked through gelatin and found the director waiting at a table on the terrace. She was a sophisticated sixtysomething with a smooth gray bob.

The meeting went well. Bernadette had already read the book that Lexi wanted to adapt and not only saw Lexi in the lead role, she had ideas for additional financing.

Lexi walked out on unsteady legs, optimistic about her career for the first time in years. As she arrived home, she received a text from her lawyer.

X-Calibur has been notified. I'll call later with details.

Also good news, but it didn't stop her from running to the toilet, where she threw up every bite of food she'd eaten.

Aside from confirming with her doctor, Lexi told no one, still in a state of denial because a baby would be such a huge life change. She couldn't understand how it had happened. Why now? *No.*

The morning sickness said yes, but for the rest of each day she was able to pretend it wasn't real, which was helpful because she couldn't fathom bringing a baby into this messy life of hers. Hadley was making a quiet fuss, trying to woo her back, but at least he wasn't taking it to the public sphere.

That threat of a scandal and a spotlight would always be present in her life, though, which meant any children she had would also live under a microscope.

Actors might bring babies onto sets these days, but she knew the downfall of growing up on one.

She also knew parenting was *hard*. Her mother had always had ample funds, thanks to support payments from Lexi's father, but she had struggled in other ways. And Lexi knew for a fact that the most serene, sentimental moments of a mother holding a baby on film were achieved after hours of waiting for that baby to stop screaming its lungs out.

Parenting was not as easy and romantic as it was portrayed. This was a terrible time for her to become one.

She was pro-choice all the way so she didn't feel she *had* to have the baby, but each time she considered not having it, she couldn't hold on to the thought.

When Bernadette invited her to stay with her at her home in Nice, and said, "One of my regular investors is in Monte Carlo. You can help me charm him," Lexi eagerly went.

Filming was at least two years away. Her pregnancy wouldn't be a factor, but Lexi wanted to look for a new home. France had stricter privacy laws than the US and there were some very discreet maternity clinics in Switzerland.

She might be telling herself she hadn't made a decision, but she was making decisions as though she had decided.

What would Magnus say about her having his baby, she wondered? She would hide her pregnancy as long as possible, but once paparazzi got wind of it, they would speculate the baby was his. She had to warn him before that.

She wasn't ready to face him, though. Their night haunted her, sparking every emotion from erotic thrill to wistful longing to the ache of rejection. The only thing she couldn't seem to feel was regret.

Did he regret their affair? He might, once he learned about the baby. Would he blame her? Accuse her of orchestrating this? They'd been *his* condoms that he had applied. It wasn't her fault they'd failed.

Oh, she *dreaded* telling him she was pregnant. That was the real reason she was pretending it wasn't actually happening.

She would tell him when she had all the pieces in place to raise this baby alone, because that's what she planned to do. Yes. She had decided.

Then she walked into a cocktail party in Monte Carlo and there he was.

As a teen, Magnus had aspired to become an Olympic athlete, but he'd always seen the tech industry as his eventual career. Thanks to Katla's strategic marriage, Isleif was a growing hub of innovation. Magnus was continuing what Prince Sorr had started by attending trade conferences and high-level summits around every aspect of tech, most lately the impacts of AI, but he was also tasked with encouraging multinational tech companies to set up shop in Isleif.

Many heads of such conglomerates had homes in Monte Carlo, the most expensive real estate in the world. Going to a party there provided casual introductions and it was also a suitable place for a first date with the woman at the top of Ulmer's list of suitable brides.

Lady Annalise was visiting her cousin in Monaco, a woman who had married into the royal family here. Annalise ticked all the boxes for a future queen: she was a blue-blooded philanthropist, cultured, and had no troublesome scandals in her history. She was stylish and had a quick wit and knew how high-society games were played. She was not averse to moving to a tiny country in the North Atlantic. In fact, their marriage had the potential to strengthen ties with the royal family here in Monaco as well as her highly placed relatives in Denmark.

Magnus really wanted to feel something for her, but she left him stone cold.

They were standing on the terrace of a villa, listening to someone drone on about winning a painting at an auction when Magnus felt the air change. *Charge*. It was as though a thunderstorm gathered, but the sky remained clear and the breeze stayed soft.

He swiveled his head to the party inside and took an invisible kick to his gut.

Lexi. She stood at the top of the three shallow steps that led from the foyer into the columned living room. She was looking to the right while leaned down to hear the chic, gray-haired woman beside her.

Someone moved and Magnus was able to see her gown was an ethereal blue that looked as though it had been designed by the ancient Greeks. Its one-shoulder style was held up by braided silver cord against her golden skin. A matching band underscored her generous breasts while the skirt fell in a graceful curtain that hid the navel he'd kissed. The hips he'd bracketed with his hands. The thighs he'd pushed apart, then felt grip his waist.

He never allowed himself to search her name, even though she was top of mind from the moment he woke and through his colorless days, then into his fitful, erotic dreams. The few times he had broken down for a glimpse of her, all he saw were trolls and clickbait nonsense. That made him furious on her behalf, which brought on a wave of guilt because, for a few minutes that morning in Paris, *he* had thought the worst of her.

Aside from early attempts by the press to link them, however, she had managed to quash speculation that they were romantically involved.

Being a card-carrying hypocrite, he was quietly furious about that, too. He wanted her to betray some hint that she was as obsessed as he was. Because he still wanted her. She was an itch within him he couldn't scratch, one that was driving him mad.

His blood caught fire as he stared at her through the crowd.

She nodded at her friend, then cast her gaze around the party—and froze. Her pink lips parted in shock before she abruptly looked down at the steps and melted into the crowd.

There was a ripple of laughter in the people around him so he pulled his attention back to the conversation even as Annalise excused them, saying she was cold and wanted to step inside.

"Did you already know the punchline of his story?" she asked as they reentered the din of the party.

"No." Magnus didn't even remember what the man had been talking about.

"Oh. I thought you were bored with them. You seemed to check out on us. That's why I said we should come in."

What could he say? His inner beast was off-leash, stalking the crowd for—

"Oh, look! It's Paisley Pockets!" Annalise clutched his arm with subdued excitement.

No. His adrenaline surged and he followed her gaze, locking on Lexi, but whatever came into his face made Annalise sober.

"You didn't like her show? It's all I watched growing up. I *loved* it." Her tone panged with nostalgia.

"Are you referring to Lexi Alexander?" He glanced again in Lexi's direction, trying to sound disinterested while swallowing her with his eyes.

She had her back to him. Her hair was loosely braided. The tail sat between shoulder blades that struck him as tense, even from across the room.

She's been in trouble with the law.

That's what he should have said, but he couldn't bring himself to denigrate her. To gossip like a busybody neighbor.

"Would you like to meet her?" He was being *polite*.

"You know her?" Annalise brightened with curiosity.

"We met briefly in Paris earlier this year." It had been brief. Too brief.

"Will you think me ridiculous if I say yes?"

She didn't know the meaning of the word. This was *absurd*, but he took her across the room to where Lexi was speaking to the gray-haired woman and a heavy-set man.

Lexi was an exceptional actress because, after the slightest stiffening of shock, she beamed with courtesy and welcome.

"Your Royal Highness." Her gaze flickered over his tuxedo in a way that made him wish it was her hands before she swept her attention back to his face. "How nice to see you again."

"Ms. Alexander." He held her gaze, quietly affronted by her use of his title. He was Magnus and she was Lexi. God and goddess. Or had she forgotten? "Lady Annalise wanted to say hello."

"I was such a fan growing up," Annalise gushed, clasping both her hands around the one that Lexi offered.

"You're very kind." Lexi smoothly accepted the praise before introducing her friend, a film director, and a man in town for the high-stakes poker tournament that began tomorrow.

A lively discussion of the gamble of filmmaking ensued. As everyone bantered, Magnus waited for Lexi's gaze to come back to his, but she stubbornly looked at anyone *but* him, all while wearing a bright, engaged smile.

"When does filming start on your project?" he asked her directly.

"Oh. It's, um, not confirmed yet, so a year or two at least." Her gaze barely lifted above his bow tie and her expression remained stiff before she quickly looked to her friend. "When we do get a green light, Bernadette has a lot of work ahead of her while I—" She pressed her lips together and tucked a nonexistent strand of hair behind her ear. "My agent— My *new* agent." Her gaze finally crashed into his but veered away just as quickly. "She suggested I write a memoir before someone decides to write an unauthorized biography, so I'm on the hunt for a quiet place here in Europe to, um, do that."

Was she self-conscious about writing about herself? For anyone else it would be a vanity project, but her story of working from the time she'd been a baby was unique enough to make for an interesting read.

Everyone chimed in with location suggestions, then the man excused himself to speak to someone else.

"We should be on our way, too. We're staying in Nice and it's getting late," Lexi said, glancing at Bernadette.

They had just gotten here and it was only nine o'clock. The drive to Nice took twenty minutes, thirty if you obeyed the speed limit, but okay. After polite goodbyes, the pair of women left.

"She seems so down-to-earth. I wanted to ask her for a photo," Annalise mused.

Good God, that really would have taken this farce to a new height.

"I didn't think it was a good idea, seeing as you're involved with her."

He bristled. "What makes you say that?" It was a real question because he had been concentrating on not betraying anything and Lexi had been doing an excellent job of the same.

Annalise tucked her chin, and her mouth pinched

with admonishment. "It was like being between a pair of magnets that were turned the wrong way."

His chest hardened like concrete. At the same time, he had the darkly amusing thought that Ulmer was right. Annalise would have made him a good wife. She was observant and unwilling to put up with his BS.

"I'm not involved with her," he assured her. "It was brief and it's over."

"Is it?" she asked mildly. "If you don't mind, I'd rather leave. I don't think this will work."

He took her home and he was still brooding on her skeptical, "Is it?" an hour later when he received a text from Vijay.

Ms. Alexander said she saw you tonight in Monaco. She wonders if you have time for a coffee while you're in town.

The animal in him lurched against the chain that was strangling him. He wanted to make time. He wanted to gather a fleet of a thousand ships and storm Nice, bringing Lexi Alexander back to his bed by any means necessary.

They *were* over, though. They were impossible. If he saw her to tell her that, he would turn it into something that was liable to destroy them both.

The struggle between what he wanted and what he had to do flashed him back to those painful early days of moving into the palace at Isleif. His siblings had been as confused as he was, asking with bewilderment, "Are you ever coming home?"

It had been agony to accept that everything had

changed. The painful weight of the crown forced him to put Isleif first, tearing a rift between them that he had never been able to repair, one that continued to make him ache with loss to this day.

He knew what he had to do with Lexi. He knew it would feel as though he was amputating his own limb, but he did it anyway. He texted Vijay that same brutal word.

No.

He didn't hear from her again.

CHAPTER SIX

Vijay texted Magnus five months later.

We need to chat. In person would be better.

Aside from that one text in March that he had re-layed from Lexi, Vijay's only texts since Paris had been a monthly reassurance of "no concerns." Today should have been the seventh of those.

Not that Magnus was counting.

He was definitely counting.

Magnus prompted him.

About?

Possible vulnerability. Important. Not yet urgent.

I'm due in New York tomorrow.

I can meet you there Wednesday.

See you then.

"Is that a meeting I can take, sir?" Ulmer asked when he received the request from Vijay's assistant to firm things up. "I understood all training is up to date with the security team. Your schedule in New York is already very full. If he's merely pitching—"

"Find room. Tack it on to the end if necessary."

"We can't put off the departure time. You're due in Reykjavík Thursday."

Outwardly, Reykjavík was a diplomatic engagement. In reality, it was a covert second date between Magnus and yet another woman who did nothing for him.

"Am I correct to assume your meeting with Mr. Sahir relates to Ms. Alexander?" Ulmer pried. He'd been deeply annoyed that her presence at the party in Monaco had slipped through his otherwise Big Brother– level surveillance.

"I'll let you know once he tells me."

"Her Majesty will not be pleased."

"Then don't tell her."

Katla was tied up before he left so Magnus was able to skip any stern warnings against seeing Lexi. Ulmer was likely correct, though. Magnus had no doubt Lexi was the subject of their meeting.

Landing in New York, he pushed himself through the meetings he had scheduled, counting down the minutes until Vijay arrived at his hotel suite.

When he did, Magnus brought him onto the terrace where they could have a modicum of privacy.

"This is about Lexi?" Magnus voiced the concern that had been grating in him. "Are there new threats against her?"

"No. Her team remains vigilant, but things have settled down now that she has cut ties with her brother. He faces a defamation suit if her name passes his lips."

After she had said "my new agent," Magnus had quietly looked into her settlement from X-Calibur. It was an eyebrow-raising amount, making him think, *Good for her.*

"And her stalker?" he asked.

"She didn't want to pursue charges for his presence at the Paris hotel, but he's now on a no-fly list. He also knows we're watching his every move. If he tries to sell Ms. Alexander's likeness, it will trigger another lawsuit. It's enough of a threat that he's moved on."

"Where is she? Europe?" God, he was weak, but he had the sense she'd done exactly as she'd suggested and dropped off-grid to write her book.

"She's in Switzerland. I'm going to see her on my way back to India. She wants to settle up on the services that you've covered, then restructure her arrangement with me."

"Meaning you'll reimburse me and everything between you and Lexi becomes confidential." His gut tightened as he realized his last tie to her was about to be severed. "You mentioned a vulnerability?"

"I did." Vijay squeezed the back of his neck, betraying uncharacteristic hesitation. "I've struggled with how much to tell you. I discussed it with Killian, actually," he said, referring to the owner of TecSec. "He said he had a similar situation once. In that case, his mandate was to protect the entire family so the ethics were clear-cut. In this case, Ms. Alexander gave me permission to share pertinent details with you, but my problem is that I can't be one hundred percent certain this detail is pertinent to *you*."

"I am a busy man, Vijay," Magnus reminded him with a roll of his wrist.

"She asked me to prepare a quote for additional security. For the baby, once it arrives."

"The—" Magnus had only experienced this complete blankness once before in his life, when Ulmer had said to him, *It's our belief that your father is not your biological father.*

A strange, searing pain arrived at the periphery of his awareness. A recognition of a truth that was too painful to accept, one that would blind him when it was allowed in so he mentally held it off, staying safely inside a bubble of disbelief. Denial. It wasn't real. He'd misheard.

A thousand years and less than a minute passed.

Slowly he became aware of being on the terrace in New York. The sun was on his shoulders. City sounds were far below. Vijay's expression hadn't changed, but an acidic burn of betrayal began to seep into his bloodstream.

"It's mine?" he asked in a rasp.

"She didn't say." Vijay pushed his hands into his pockets, expression turning circumspect. "I felt you should be informed regardless, since assumptions will be made that it is. She wants everything in place two weeks before her due date. The math from the end of October calculates back to conception in January, about the time we all met in Paris."

"Math." You couldn't argue with math, could you?

"Take your time. My first was unplanned. I know how it scrambles the jets."

"It can't be mine," Magnus blurted.

He had used condoms. He was supposed to marry someone appropriate. Katla would have him flayed alive in the town square. He might chafe at her lectures and Ulmer's interference, but he understood the stakes. He needed to continue Katla's efforts to repair the royal family's image, not prove he was his father's son by having an illegitimate baby—

This was why he used condoms!

But he had a memory of drifting in the twilight of postorgasmic bliss, exhausted by lovemaking, then lurching awake to a strange sensation. The condom was slipping as his erection faded.

He'd hardened as he'd awakened still inside her. That damned woman seemed to keep him in a perpetual state of erection. He was twitching with arousal just thinking of her and their night of sensual debauchery.

The rush of erotic memory was countered by a cooler thought, though. Had the condom slipped enough to fail? Even if it had, that didn't automatically mean he was the father. She could have slept with a dozen men before and after him.

Even as he had that thought, he recalled how frightened she'd been that night in Paris, after seeing her stalker. How angry she'd been when she'd said, *You're accusing me of staging this?*

And he could still hear her admitting in the shadows of his bedroom, *I don't do this.*

He ran his hand down his face, giving his beard a

tug hard enough to hurt, grounding himself into this new reality.

"She's keeping it." Obviously. She was seven months along and making arrangements for the baby's protection. "This will be a PR nightmare. But that's the least of it, isn't it?"

"If the baby is yours, broader decisions become necessary, yes," Vijay said evenly. "I'm here to assist any way that I can."

If the baby was his? Magnus knew it was. That's why she had looked so damned uncomfortable when she had told him she was going into hiding to write her memoir. That's why his brain was exploding.

Secrets had been kept from him *again*.

Lexi covered where the baby was pressing a foot against the side wall of her round belly and smiled while trying not to yearn for the baby's father to experience it with her.

How could she want to see him when she was still so mad at him?

The prince is unavailable.

That was what Vijay had texted back the night after she'd seen Magnus in Monte Carlo five months ago.

Because he'd been on a date with Lady Annalise?

God, it had hurt to see him with someone else. It had taken her very best acting to pretend she was unbothered by the sight of them together, and to claim that she was "always happy to speak with a fan," and that Portugal did sound like a wonderful place to hole up and write a book.

He had been horrible to her that morning in Paris and he stood there pretending nothing had ever happened between them at all while she had thought her pregnancy must be obvious to everyone. How could it not be?

As much as she had dreaded telling him, her conscience had demanded she reach out.

The arrogant jerk refused to see her.

Devastated by his fresh rejection, she hadn't pressed it. Had that been cowardly? Sure. Mostly, she'd been embarrassed at having asked to see him at all. She had felt like one of those needy women who couldn't take a hint that a man wasn't interested. She had never, ever wanted to be the sort of woman who couldn't live without a man, yet she felt like one. Or rather, she felt sometimes as though she couldn't live without that particular man.

When he had rebuffed her again, she had made herself move on to prove that she could. She seized his refusal to see her as an excuse to delay telling him about the baby, sold her mansion in California and leased a flat in Zurich until she began to show. Then she moved into this private clinic where she wrote between swimming and yoga and birthing classes.

She didn't love regurgitating her past for financial gain, but the generous advance had been a nice boon while she'd been waiting on Hadley's settlement. He had paid a pretty penny for her shares in X-Calibur and included an additional settlement to avoid a forensic audit and an investigation into his PR practices.

Lexi would always be sad that things had ended on

such a sour note with him and Janet. In her heart of hearts, she had always hoped she and her father's children would develop a closer bond, but there was something cathartic in letting go of that dream as she started her own family with her baby.

Now that was finalized, she could settle up with Vijay—and Magnus. Then, and only then, would she insist Magnus speak to her so she could tell him about the baby.

She wouldn't let his dating life get in her way, either. Yes, she looked him up often enough to know he was wining and dining every eligible heiress around the globe—amid rumors that he was in search of a wife. That stung, too. And if he'd seemed serious about any of them, she might have felt guiltier about keeping him in the dark, but as he was photographed in various places with various women, her pride had hardened her silence around their baby. *Her* baby.

After today, however, she would be out of Magnus's debt. She had put an offer in on a house in France where she and her baby would reside when not on set. Between the book she was writing, and the movie, and other investments, she had enough income to raise their child without Magnus's involvement.

It will be fine, she kept telling herself.

Her baby didn't need a close relationship with its father. She hadn't had one. Not at first. Her father hadn't wanted anything to do with her until her career had taken off and, frankly, she would have been better off if he'd stayed out of her life.

So she could almost convince herself there would be

a bright side if Magnus preferred to hide the fact he'd fathered her child.

It would hurt, though. It would crush her on their baby's behalf.

But she and the baby would be fine. Somehow, someway. She would make sure of it.

She checked the time. Almost ten. She made her way to the foyer, where Vijay would have to wait for her since guests were discouraged within the residential part of the clinic, to protect the privacy of its wealthy, high-profile clientele.

The clinic was a beautiful chalet-style building situated above a quiet village in the Alps, one that could easily be mistaken for an upscale spa with its kidney-shaped pool and serenity garden and five-star chef. It had treatment rooms for massage, a gym and three very well-equipped exam rooms, plus two birthing suites and an emergency OR. Between the midwife, the nutritionist and her doctor, Lexi was being very well cared for.

The receptionist was on the phone, but she held up two fingers, then pointed down the hall, indicating Vijay was waiting in room two of the visitor parlors.

Lexi nodded and turned the corner, surprised to see Vijay outside the closed door.

"Ms. Alexander," he greeted politely as she approached. "How are you feeling?"

"Fine. You?"

"Fine, but mine was a real question. Is everything going well? No high blood pressure or other concerns that could affect our meeting?"

"My back hurts when I sit too long. And I'm getting

to the stage where I need the powder room constantly," she added wryly.

He didn't crack a smile, only nodded gravely.

"I'll use it before we start. I believe there's one in there." She pointed at the door he had yet to open.

"I need to explain something before we go in. When we started our arrangement in Paris, you agreed—"

The door was abruptly pulled inward, creating a vacuum that nearly pulled her soul from her body and into the towering figure that blocked the opening.

Magnus. He was broader and more imposing than she remembered. Angrier.

Lexi had an impression of a dark suit and a green tie and a sensation of all the blood leaving her head. She watched his impossibly blue irises sweep down to her middle. An inward thump might have been a kick from their baby, but it might have been the impact of her heart landing on the floor.

His gaze came back to hers, rife with accusation.

Her vision disintegrated at the edges. Had she forgotten to breathe?

"Ms. Alexander." Vijay's hand closed tightly around her upper arm.

She tried to grasp on to him, but her limbs had turned to overcooked pasta. A ringing sound filled her ears—

The sight of Lexi's undeniably pregnant figure was still hitting him when Magnus realized her color had drained. Her eyelids fluttered and her eyeballs rolled back.

Vijay was already starting to catch her, but Magnus reacted in a flash, stepping out to gather her crumpling form. If she'd gained any weight since the last time he'd held her, he didn't feel it. So much adrenaline was firing through his veins, he could have lifted her over his head and carried her across the continent. She felt no heavier than a long winter coat draped limply over his arms.

"I told you to let me warn her," Vijay snapped, as Magnus carried her to the sofa. "I'll get someone."

"You were taking too long," Magnus muttered, but the door was already closing.

Patience was not in his wheelhouse. That's why Magnus had insisted on accompanying Vijay to this clinic. When he'd heard the murmur of her voice beyond the door, he had wanted the answers he'd come here for.

He hadn't meant to startle her so badly she fainted. He forgot sometimes that he was such a big man. She was tall and lean, but flexible and strong. He had remembered her as assertive and surprisingly adept at rolling with punches.

In his mind, he'd begun to believe she was using this pregnancy as a form of extortion. By the time they'd landed in Zurich, he'd worked himself into seeing her as a threat and arrived ready to fight.

She was pregnant, though. Delicate? As he lifted her head to adjust the cushion beneath it, he noted the soft curve of her cheek, the shadows beneath her eyes.

"Lexi?" He hitched his hip beside hers and set two fingers in her throat where her pulse was strong, if uneven. She was breathing, but her lips were colorless. Her hand was lax when he picked it up.

The door opened and a fresh surge of protectiveness had him standing to face the intruder.

It was a woman in a white lab coat with a stethoscope hung around her neck. Vijay came in behind her and closed the door.

"I'm Dr. Rivera. Can you tell me what happened?" She barely looked at Magnus as she brushed him aside and gave Lexi's sternum a rub. "Lexi?"

Lexi winced and twitched away from the light that the doctor shone into her eyes.

"It's Dr. Rivera, Lexi. Are you in pain?"

"No," she murmured, blinking her eyes open. "What hap—Oh." She saw Magnus and turned her face to the back of the couch.

"Do you want me to ask these men to leave?" Dr. Rivera asked.

"How many are there?" Lexi looked around, then said sullenly to Vijay, "Are you planning to ambush me with anyone else? My brother? My dead father, perhaps?"

"Don't be angry with Vijay." Magnus stayed behind the doctor where he could see that color was returning to her lips. "I wanted to see you and didn't give him a choice."

"I'm not giving you a choice, either." Dr. Rivera straightened and looped her stethoscope behind her neck. "Stay here while I get a wheelchair. I want you in an exam room while we check a few things. Oxygen, glucose. We'll put the fetal heart monitor on you, to be sure everything is as it should be. No stress please, gentlemen."

"I apologize, Ms. Alexander," Vijay said as the doctor left. "This wasn't how I wanted to handle this. At all." He glowered at Magnus.

"Leave us," Magnus said.

No one ever defied him, but Vijay folded his arms and said, "Ms. Alexander?"

"It's fine. I was going to ask you today if you could contact him for me." Her voice was quiet and heavy.

As the door closed behind Vijay, Lexi started to sit up.

Magnus pressed her shoulder into the sofa cushion. "The doctor said don't move."

"I can sit up." She tried to brush his hand off her, but he only caught it, keeping the weight of his fingertips against the hollow of her shoulder.

He was still unsettled by her faint. Her cool hand twitched in his grip before she twisted it free. Her brow flexed and she bit her bottom lip, gaze skating toward the back of the sofa again.

Reluctantly, he straightened so they were no longer touching.

"Why did you want to speak to me?" he asked.

Lexi released a humorless choke and looked toward the basketball that was her waistline.

"Mine." It wasn't really a question. It was more something that washed through him like a visceral sensation.

Not that he'd had any real doubt. No, the greater surprise was the nature of this feeling that swept through him. It wasn't a cold chill, the way he'd felt when he'd been told his father was really King Einer. When that had happened, a bleak weight had fallen on him, one that had severed him from his old life and left him sick with loss.

This was the opposite. His life had flipped again, reordering everything he believed to be true. A similar crushing sense of responsibility crashed over him, but this time it expanded a force within him. Strength pulsed through him. Determination. *Fire*.

Why? Everything about this was wrong, especially the part where he was becoming a father. What the hell did he know about parenting? Neither of the two men he referred to as his father had given him a good example to follow. They'd each cut him adrift in their own way, leaving him floundering in strange waters, abandoned and questioning his self-worth.

Yet he was the father of Lexi's baby. He had a thousand pressing matters that he'd disregarded to come here and all he could wonder was *Where is that damned doctor?* He needed to know the baby was okay. That Lexi was.

"You're not happy," Lexi said heavily.

He hadn't been happy, truly happy, since he'd beat his own record on a giant slalom the day he'd turned eighteen. Things had gone downhill even faster than he had, once Ulmer had introduced himself, but at least that memory reminded him what needed to be done as the doctor returned with the wheelchair.

"Let's get you down the hall for your tests," Dr. Rivera said to Lexi.

"Add one more," Magnus said. "Paternity."

He didn't believe the baby was his.

She shouldn't be surprised. Or insulted. But she was both.

Lexi agreed to have blood drawn for the paternity test along with the rest. A nurse helped her change into a hospital gown and she answered all the questions about what she had eaten today, submitted to various pokes and prods, then tried to relax while the monitor recorded the baby's heart rate.

It wasn't easy. Every time she closed her eyes, she saw the thunderous expression on Magnus's face when he had pulled open that door.

"They said I could come in as long as I don't upset you." He walked in with the energy of a caged lion and closed the door behind him.

She suppressed her jump of surprise, but decided she would rather get this discussion over with than sit in pre-performance jitters, feeling as though she was waiting to go on a talk show for a six-minute mea culpa.

He had removed his suit jacket and wore a pin in his tie over a crisp white shirt. His hair was smoothly pulled back, his brows low with consternation. His shoulders were *so* broad. Everything about him screamed power, intimidating her, yet she reacted in a potently sexual way, too. She was accosted by memories of his lips pressing her skin, his wide hand between her thighs. His body surging over hers while lightning gathered in her belly.

She tried to swallow and looked to the pastoral painting on the wall, pretending that her cheeks weren't stinging with a bloom of sexual heat.

"You're the one who's upset," she said stiffly. "I hope you believe me when I say I didn't mean for this to happen."

"The responsibility is mine. I never should have touched you."

Oh, Gawd. His disdainful tone made her shrivel inside.

"Why am I the last to know?" he asked in that same aloof voice.

"No one knows you're the father. Only a handful of medical professionals know I'm pregnant and Vijay only knows where I am because I asked him to meet me here. I wanted to clear my debt with you before I told you so you'll believe me when I say I'm not asking for anything from you. By hiding my pregnancy, I can say the baby was born by surrogate and keep you out of it completely."

"Am I supposed to be comforted by that?" His tone was even, but she heard the roil of emotion beneath it.

"I knew this wouldn't be welcome news," she said shakily, touching where the baby was giving a reassuringly strong kick at the top of her belly. "I know the challenges I'll face if we acknowledge this baby is yours. We *both* have a vested interest in keeping your name out of it."

Her deliberate use of his words landed on target because he narrowed his eyes.

"You're deluding yourself," he said flatly. "On several fronts. That baby is going to come out at five kilos wearing a horned hat. There won't be any doubt that it's mine."

"I...don't know how much that is."

"Big."

She was afraid of that. Had literally been worrying about it.

Magnus muttered something under his breath and flexed his hands.

"This is me keeping my temper so I don't upset you as I explain why I'm very angry that you kept this from me," he said in a tone that was exaggerated in its evenness.

"My body, my choice, Magnus."

"Agreed," he cut in, still with that suppressed emotion suffusing his deep voice. "I appreciate that pregnancy is a huge decision. You needed time to consider whether you wanted to continue with it. Fine. Hiding the pregnancy from the rest of the world is also fine. Hiding it from me strikes a very raw, personal nerve."

"I tried to meet you in Monte Carlo," she reminded in a hiss.

"You didn't try very hard," he snapped back.

She couldn't argue that so she didn't bother.

"I told you I never met my father. My biological father," he clarified. "Everything about my relationship to him was kept from me until it was thrown in my face on my eighteenth birthday."

"By whom?"

"Ulmer. He found me at a ski hill, showed me some identification and asked to speak with me. My mother was born on Isleif. She still had family there. I thought he was going to tell me someone we knew had died. Instead, he told me Queen Katla was approaching forty and was childless. She feared she would be the end of the Thorolf line so she was forced to determine whether I was her bastard half brother."

"He didn't call you that." Ulmer knew how to make a person feel small, but he didn't resort to insults. Did he?

"It quickly became obvious that's what I was," Magnus stated with a sweep of his hand through the air. "My mother wasn't married when I was conceived, only engaged to the man I came to believe was my father, Sveyn. She genuinely didn't know who the father was, but she feared the palace would take me if I turned out to be the king's. She talked Sveyn into moving to Norway."

"Did she tell *him*?"

"No. King Einer was killed six years later. By then Katla was married and trying for an heir. My mother thought it would never come up again."

"Sveyn never questioned it? Did you? Do you look like him?"

"Enough. We're all tall with similar coloring. I thought Ulmer was delusional when he said what he did. I consented to the blood test because it seemed the quickest way to make him go away. Within a few hours I was confronting my mother, blindsiding Sveyn in the process."

A chill settled into Lexi's chest. She bunched a handful of the sheet that covered her legs, feeling the anger and betrayal coming off him as waves of icy gales and scorching heat, understanding that some of that was directed at her, for hiding this baby from him.

"That must have been a difficult moment for all of you," she murmured.

"It broke their marriage," he said starkly. "Sveyn left. I haven't spoken to him since. For years after, my brother and sister barely spoke to me."

"They blamed you?" She flashed a look up at his grim expression.

"They didn't know what to think of me. Everything

we had in common, everything we believed about our family, was a lie. I had to move to Isleif so I wasn't there to… Hell, I don't even know what my side of it was, only that no one cared to hear it."

Her heart felt squeezed in a giant fist. "Magnus—"

"It's water under the bridge," he said bluntly. "What I'm saying is, I would never do something like that to my own child. I wouldn't hide their parent from them. That's why this—" he waved a finger to take in the clinic and her pregnancy "—infuriates me."

"I understand." And she hurt for the young man he'd been. It explained so much about how remote he was, walking around as though infused with the force of a hurricane. "But I didn't know any of that. And if we're talking childhoods, let me explain where I'm coming from. When *my* mother got pregnant, my father shuffled her off to Arizona and resentfully paid her support, angry that she insisted on having me. I was six when I realized I was the reason we had nice things, and that other little girls didn't play house on film sets every day. It was only when my career began to take off that my father showed an interest in me. Once he got involved on the contract side, the pressure to work really hit. And when Paisley Pockets became a hit, Mom and Dad got into a huge custody battle that had everything to do with the value of my renewal contract and nothing to do with *me*."

She glanced at the monitor to ensure that her strident voice and climb in temperature wasn't affecting the baby.

"*I* want this baby. It had to be my decision and I had

to know I could raise it alone. You think I don't know how it looks? Your first thought had to be that I plotted to have the baby of a rich man. Don't deny it." She waved an accusing finger at him. "But that's not what this is. I need you to believe that. I was waiting until I was in a position to *not* need you before I told you."

"I don't think that's true."

"I'm not lying to you!" She dropped her hand to her side.

"No, you're lying to yourself." He glanced with concern at the monitor. "You wanted to cement yourself into a life where you can raise this baby alone because you knew what would happen as soon as you told me."

Her heart lurched and she splayed both hands on her bump. "You're not taking this baby from me, Magnus."

"Of course not. I just explained why it's paramount to me that my child knows both their parents from their first breath. No. For such a smart, ambitious, level-headed woman, you have been remarkably naive, Lexi. I can only assume it's fear. You're not wrong to be frightened. It's a hellish life you chose for both of you when you decided to have that baby. But you did."

"No, Magnus." She dug her heels into the mattress, pushing her back into the pillows because she sensed whatever he was going to say would be too big to withstand.

His flinty gaze flickered to the monitor and he seemed to choose his words carefully.

"I wish things were different, Lexi. I do. But that's not just any baby. You knew that the moment you found out you were pregnant. That's why you've been hiding it. You didn't want to admit what that means."

"It doesn't have to mean anything. That's what I'm saying. You don't—" Hot-cold shivers of premonition were washing over her. "You don't have to be involved." She forced the words through her tight throat, but they came out high and desperate. Panicked. "This is *my* baby. My body. My *life*. *I* decide what happens to me. To us."

He said nothing, only looked at her with pity in his expression. *Pity.*

Goose bumps rose on her arms and prickled down her back. Her whole life had been fishtailing on ice since she had learned of her pregnancy. No, since she had first locked eyes with him. She had thought she had begun taking control over the last months, but now a cliff seemed to loom before her, offering nothing but a huge, foggy void that she was about to plummet into.

"No, Magnus," she whispered.

"I have a duty to produce the next ruler, Lexi. Preferably within the sanctity of marriage, but that part has been overlooked before." His lip curled with cynicism.

"I'm not marrying you."

He snorted.

"You don't want to marry me," she hurried to continue. "You didn't even want to talk to me five months ago. The morning after, even!"

"Lexi—"

"No. It would be a disaster. *You know that.*" Her throat grew hot and so did the backs of her eyes. "Your people won't accept me. Your queen won't. No to everything you're saying. *No.*"

"Do you think I didn't try saying that when it happened to me?" Maybe if he had sounded patronizing, she wouldn't have welled up, but he sounded *sorry* for her.

"I'm not unreasonable, Magnus." She was in a fight for her life. Her heart rate picked up and tension gripped her. "I will grant you some say over what happens to our baby, but you don't get to make decisions for *me.*"

"I'm not making these decisions, Lexi." He didn't raise his voice, but it rang with power all the same.

She was trying to sink through the pillows behind her, through the exam table and into the floor. Anything to escape the invisible force that seemed to emanate out of him, pushing against her like the wall of a bubble that was going to break only enough to pull her inside it where she would be trapped forever.

She couldn't breathe, not enough to speak. Not enough to tell him to quit talking.

"History is making this decision for both of us. People think rulers rule, but we are ruled by precedent and necessity and duty. There are perks. The royal chest can buy you all the nice things you want. Every physical need you have will be amply met from now on. What is unaffordable to me, however, and to you, is choice. We are bound by duty to the crown."

"You might be." She reached for a tissue and blew her nose. "I'm not. Not to your ruler or your rules. I'm not…"

"Lexi. It's done. Unless that paternity test comes back

with a negative, we started down this path in Paris. There is no fork in the road now."

"There *is*," she insisted, but her lips were quivering too much for her to say more.

"I'm upsetting you." He came close enough to cup her cheek and set the pad of this thumb against her trembling mouth. "Believe me when I say I know exactly how you feel. You put up a good fight and I admire you for it. It reassures me that you'll weather what's coming. But save your strength for other fights because this one is over."

"It's not." The tears brimming her eyes overflowed, infuriating her because she wasn't a weak woman. "I have a p-plan."

"Cry if you need to." He reached for a tissue and dried each of her cheeks, expression dispassionate. "But accept it. I'm taking you to Isleif and we're going to marry. I have to tell the queen."

He walked out, leaving her with a scream of frustration caught in her throat.

CHAPTER SEVEN

MAGNUS RECOGNIZED THE irony in telling Lexi to accept their situation when he was still wavering between denial and anger himself, wondering if the paternity test would let him off the hook.

He didn't want it to. That was the truth. Beneath the rubble of this disaster was a pulse of anticipation. Lexi would be his, whether she was prepared to accept it or not. She wasn't wrong that her reputation was inconvenient, but the rest was tremendously convenient. Now he could have a wife who lit his sexual fire.

And yes, that fact was hellishly dangerous, considering that giving in to his lust for her had put him in this life-altering position in the first place, but he still reveled in it.

Outside her exam room, he found two of his own guards waiting for him. They must have come in with Ulmer. Magnus had asked Vijay to release Ulmer from the purgatory of waiting in the car. He and Vijay were now in the room where Magnus had been shown when they arrived. Ulmer was tapping his tablet, as usual. Both men stood as Magnus entered.

"Did you tell the queen?" Magnus asked Ulmer.

"Her Majesty is aware there has been a detour." He still sounded frosted by it, even though it had been a solid ten hours since Magnus had ordered it. "I told her that explanations are best coming from you."

"You know why we're here, though." Magnus looked to Vijay, who kept his lips sealed and shook his head, indicating he hadn't said a word.

"The service this clinic offers, and Mr. Sahir's presence, speak for themselves." Ulmer looked to his tablet. "Mr. Sahir and I have been running potential scenarios, projecting to a time when you might have a family to protect."

By the time they left this facility, for instance. Ulmer might be a stuffy pain in Magnus's behind, but he was very good at his job.

"Ulmer and the rest of our team can take it from here," Magnus told Vijay. "One of my men can drive you to the airport."

"I'll find my own way. But may I offer you my congratulations, sir?" Vijay extended his hand.

It was a very normal thing to say to someone expecting a child, but Magnus was thrown by it. Every one of his thoughts from the moment he'd learned that Lexi was pregnant had been around how to mitigate this disaster. Even Lexi had said, *I knew this wouldn't be welcome news.*

Now, without irony, Vijay shook his hand and wished him the best, as though Magnus's impending parenthood was something to be celebrated. Not in the darkest corners of his heart because it meant he could trap Lexi into marriage, but because a new life was on its way.

Magnus thanked him, still dumbfounded, and Vijay left.

"I trust Ms. Alexander is well?" Ulmer said.

"Well enough." He'd made her faint and cry. He had not said *Thank you.* Or *I'm sorry.*

Magnus steeled himself against self-hatred because mercy was also not a luxury he could afford to offer either of them. There was no escape from who he was. He knew that better than anyone, so he didn't flinch from doing the other thing that he already knew would hurt a woman who didn't deserve it.

"Stay," he said to Ulmer as he called the palace secretary. "The queen is expecting my call," he said when Yngvar answered.

Katla's voice came on, crisp and wary. "Yes?"

"An heir is on its way, as requested."

Her breath hissed in. "Not—"

"Yes," he stated. "Lexi is due in October."

"Paternity is confirmed?"

"Not yet. But it's mine."

There was a long pause, then, "Keep this confidential. Send me the results as soon as they're available." She kept her voice steady and impassive, but Magnus knew this was a blow. For her, decades of trying had resulted in nothing but heartbreak, whereas his casually strewn oats had sown in one stolen night.

An apology rose to his tongue, but he wasn't sorry. Not nearly as sorry as he ought to be.

"You're on your way home?" she asked.

"Once the doctor confirms she can travel, yes."

"I'll see you soon." She ended the call.

* * *

Lexi was pronounced healthy and released from the exam room only for Magnus to call her into the visitor room where Ulmer also waited.

"I've settled your bill and procured a nurse to travel with us," Ulmer told her, barely glancing up from his tablet. "The dining room will prepare an early lunch for you while I pack your things. What would you like to wear for travel?" He gave her sundress a squint, deciding, "I'll leave out something appropriate for you."

"Why on earth would you help me go to Isleif?" Lexi asked him with a catch of askance laughter. "You *hate* me."

"I apologize if I gave you that impression, Ms. Alexander." Ulmer was nothing but smooth equanimity as he lowered his tablet and gave her his full, polite attention. "Please tell me how I can make that up to you. Your health and comfort are of paramount importance to me."

Lexi choked, then sent Magnus a look of disbelief, unable to find words.

"You see?" Magnus said mildly. "Even Ulmer doesn't have a choice. He has to be nice to you, now that you're a member of the royal family."

"But I'm *not*. And I don't intend to become one."

"Let's talk about that while we eat." Magnus escorted her to the dining room where they were seated in a sunny corner in an otherwise empty room.

Exasperated, she looked over her shoulder, suspecting Ulmer was gaining access to her suite despite her lack of permission for him to do so.

"Look, I accept that the baby deserves to know their father." She was trying to sound reasonable but also in charge. "Your having a say in our child's life was always on the table."

"Good. I want my child born in Isleif. All of Isleif will want their future ruler to be born there."

"I—" She clacked her teeth shut, feeling outmaneuvered. With a jerky nod, she said, "I can see that. But it doesn't mean I need to go there now. It doesn't mean we have to marry."

"We'll go there now because you've been cleared to travel. That could change as things progress. I had plans, too, you know." He waited until they'd been served cucumber water and a wedge salad before he continued. "Before I learned who I was, I aspired to ski in the Olympics. The minute I arrived at the palace, Katla told me that racing was too risky for a future king. I had to give it up. Where are you at with this film of yours?"

"If you're about to suggest I give that up, you'll hear another hard no." She had worked too hard for this chance to revive her career.

The truth was, however, acting was something she did because she was good at it and it provided the income she needed. As an art form, it allowed her to temporarily reinvent herself into someone else so she could escape the messiness of her real life, but she had often wished there was another way she could make her living that didn't cost so much of her soul.

Not that she was willing to confess that to Magnus.

"The film is based on a book about a sex worker,

isn't it?" he asked. "That's not an ideal topic for someone taking on the role of my wife."

"Oh, is your wife a *role*? Why didn't you say so? Is
there a script I could read before I commit? What's my
character like? What's my motivation?" She blinked
with facetious interest.

"I understand your resentment, but you'll have to
let it go." Magnus let his eyelids droop to a bored half-
mast. "It's not appropriate to take things out on staff.
Ulmer and I play a game of tit for tat, but he won't be
able to retaliate with you. I won't allow it. Take a swipe
at the queen at your own peril. She'll find a way to pun-
ish you that won't allow me to take the fall. That leaves
bickering with me and that's not a healthy way for us
to behave as parents."

A sting of helplessness rose behind her breastbone.
She had weathered difficult times before. She had always found a way to move forward. To retrench and
rebuild.

This was different. This wasn't a case of checking
her contract and threatening to quit if it wasn't followed
to the letter. She had a baby to think of.

Magnus was thinking of their baby, too, in his way.
He might not be acting like the most lovingly engaged
father in the world, but he didn't want their child to be
harmed the way he had been when he'd learned the truth
about his own paternity. She had to respect his desire to
be part of their baby's life. But marriage?

"Look, I will concede to going to Isleif to have the
baby. Okay? But surely we can wait on marrying? See
how we feel?" She used her most reasonable tone.

"Our marriage is for your protection, Lexi. If I have any tips on navigating what you're about to face, it's to grab any power that you're offered."

"That sounds horribly calculating. Is that really how it is for you?"

"Often enough that you should get used to it," he said drily. The pensive tension around his mouth told her he wasn't joking. Not really.

"I don't want to get married, Magnus. Not like this."

"Like what? For the sake of our baby? What would you rather? Something romantic? A declaration of love?" He was looking bored again.

"No, actually. I don't care about that." She did, though. She blindly stared out to the glare on the pool, thinking she had always wanted someone to love her. Her. Not Paisley Pockets or the girl in the bikini or any of the other roles she had played.

Her baby would love her, but could Magnus? Ever?

She had her doubts and she refused to hitch her life to something so futile.

"I'm not a romantic. I haven't been allowed to be." She chased a cherry tomato with her fork. "I've always been a product. A vehicle for someone else to make money on. My own parents did it." She shrugged that off, even though it was one of her deepest agonies. "People seek me out because I can make an introduction, or I'm a stepping stone to raise a fan's profile online. The love I receive is always superficial, but the transactions around it give me something—income or free publicity or a favor I can call in later. Marrying you gets me nothing. In fact, I would lose my identity to a man who doesn't even want me."

"We're talking about Monte Carlo again?" He hadn't finished his salad, but he pushed it aside.

"You only spoke to me because your friend wanted to meet me." The creak in her voice was humiliating, but she pressed on. "You refused to see me when I asked, but the minute you learned about this—" she waved at her middle "—you want to marry me. Do you have any idea how debasing that is? How unimportant I feel?"

"Yes." He didn't move, didn't blink. "As someone who carries DNA that forces me to live a life I didn't want, yes. I completely understand your bitterness."

Oh, she wanted to hate him for his cool logic and supreme detachment. At the same time, she hurt for him. He must have wanted to crawl out of his own skin when he learned the truth.

"Then you understand why I don't want to be your wife."

"Princess," he corrected drily. "Queen, eventually."

"Now you're mocking me, which tells me I don't even have your respect." She pushed her own salad away.

"I'm speaking the truth. You might not think those titles have value, but they do."

She offered a distracted smile when their plates were removed, but on the inside she was a fractured mirror, everything offset and webbed with cracks.

"You said this pregnancy was your fault," she reminded him. "But I know you're suspicious of me. Do you realize that you need trust between players to make a role convincing?" Her eyes were hot, her heart heavy.

"How could I pretend we're happily married when our marriage doesn't even have the most basic foundation? We have *nothing*, Magnus."

"Lexi." He set his hands on the tablecloth between them, palms up. Then he waited patiently for her to get the message that he expected her to give him her hands.

It was pure weakness on her part, but she couldn't resist touching him.

The moment she hesitantly settled her fingers into the heat of his palms, a sensual jolt traveled up her arms and into her chest where it rang like a bell.

He closed his grip before she could reflexively pull away.

"You know what we have." He squeezed again, as though deliberately causing that jolt of power in her chest. Her breath grew tight and the spark in his gaze flew into her, setting her heart alight.

"Passion doesn't last forever," she whispered.

"Nothing does." His thumbs swept across the backs of her wrists. He might as well have caressed her from head to toe, given how her whole body felt brushed by velvet. "That's why we should enjoy it while we can."

Her pulse was skipping under the caress of his fingertips.

"I don't know—" she had to clear the rasp from her throat "—if I can do that."

The doctor had said there was no physical reason she couldn't have sex, but Lexi wasn't sure if she wanted to. She wasn't the svelte woman Magnus had lifted onto his shoulders and pinned to a wall. She felt unlike herself. Awkward and far too vulnerable to withstand that kind of intimacy, especially when she couldn't shake the feeling of being rejected. *Unwanted.*

At least, that's how she felt before he chided, "You think I didn't ask?" in a way that sent a sensual shiver down her spine. "There's no physical reason you can't." His expression sobered and he released one of her hands so he could tenderly sweep a tendril of hair behind her ear. "I'll let that be your choice, though. I'm ready when you are."

"You left it in my hands last time," she reminded him on a choke of humorless laughter, sitting back and settling her hands on her bump. "I think that's your way of absolving yourself of responsibility."

"No. I meant it when I said the fault was mine."

"I don't want anyone to be at fault." She scowled, disgruntled at his continued use of that word. "That makes it sound like this baby is a mistake and I won't call them that."

"Fair enough." He sat back, too. "I do respect you, by the way. Otherwise, I would have restarted our affair in Monte Carlo and forced you to hide it."

Her heart swerved. She searched his deepwater eyes, then shook her head with uncertainty.

"No. You had already decided in Paris that I wasn't someone you could trust." She swallowed the lump that rose into her throat as she recollected that.

"You know what I think is strange?" His brows came together in puzzlement. "You say deeply personal things about yourself so it seems like you're an open book, but your actions tell a different story. *You* don't trust *me.* That's why you don't want to marry me. You don't want to rely on me. You're terrified to trust me. Aren't you? Be honest," he warned in a hint of taunt. "So we can start building this trust we need."

"No, I don't trust you," she admitted, feeling as though the admission peeled the skin from her chest, leaving her heart exposed. "I don't trust anyone. Everyone I've ever known has let me down or betrayed me. An hour ago, the man I paid *seven figures* to protect me broke my confidence and told you I was pregnant."

"Because you didn't pay him," he said with an ironic curl of his lip. "I told him not to take your money. But I hear you." He nodded, pensive. "I'll work on it. You'll need to be in Isleif for me to do that. Are you hungry? Or should we be on our way?"

CHAPTER EIGHT

BY THE TIME they were seated in his jet, the paternity result had come in. Magnus glanced at the word *Positive* and handed the tablet back to Ulmer.

"Send it to the queen."

"I'm definitely the mother?" Lexi asked with a guileless blink.

She was seated in the recliner opposite his own. Aside from Ulmer, his staff traveled in the aft cabin, on the other side of the galley, where they were seated in rows like commercial flights. In here, Ulmer kept to his cubicle while Magnus had a sofa and a dining table, a big-screen television, and windows that tinted at the touch of a button.

There was also a door to a stateroom with a bed. It was midafternoon, but he couldn't help noticing the tension in Lexi's expression and the washed-out tone in her skin. He was frustrated by her continued resistance to marriage, but he couldn't press her too hard, not when he kept remembering the way she'd been so limp in his arms, or how emotional she'd been while she'd been hooked up to all those wires.

"I know it's a lame joke," she muttered, shifting restlessly. "Everything has been so heavy and serious. Like a military operation. Is it always like this?"

"Often enough you should get used to it."

She grimaced.

"How are you feeling? Tired?"

"Why do you ask? Do you have to be nice to me, too?" she challenged lightly.

"No."

Her eyes widened in shock.

"I'm genuinely worried about you. As soon as we level off, I'll show you to the bed so you can sleep."

"It's two o'clock in the afternoon. How long is the flight?"

"Four hours. But you'll meet the queen when we arrive. You'll want to feel rested. Also, I didn't sleep on the overnight from New York, but I'm not about to leave you slumped in a chair while I stretch out on the bed."

"Is sharing a bed another thing I don't have any choice over?"

"It's just a nap, Lexi. Unless you choose to make it into more."

"I won't," she muttered, and turned her frown of consternation to the window.

A few minutes later, however, she accompanied him into the stateroom. She didn't remove any clothing except her jacket and lay down on top of the bed in her maternity top and trousers.

He did the same, only removing his shoes and jacket, then his tie and belt before he draped a light blanket over her and joined her under it.

Did he want to reach for her? God, yes, but he was

also content—disturbingly content—to simply close his eyes with the knowledge that she was beside him.

Where she belonged.

A discreet ping woke him. The recessed lighting in the floor came on, signaling they were coming into Isleif airspace and it was time to rise.

Lexi rolled to face him, eyelids heavy with sleep. "Do you want to feel the baby move?"

A strange zing went through him. Surprise and apprehension, but also excitement?

"Is it kicking?" He reached out.

She brushed her loose top up and slid the elastic panel of her trousers down, baring her belly, then she guided his hand on the tense ball of her abdomen. Within him, something restless eased as he finally had contact with her soft skin. Her warmth.

"I wasn't sure how you felt about it," she said in a small voice. "I know this isn't what you wanted. You haven't asked about the baby."

"I asked the doctor about both of you. I'm still processing this. Making a baby was something I knew I was supposed to do at some point, but it was an abstra—"

He swore as something nudged his palm, striking Magnus like a punch to the heart. A choke of wonder left him.

"Bizarre, isn't it?" He heard the smile in her voice, but he was enraptured with the swell of her belly.

"Does it hurt?" He lightly explored, searching out more proof of life.

"Not really. Surprises me sometimes."

"All I've been thinking about is the ways I have to adjust my life, not fully realizing... All we did was have sex, Lexi. Now you're growing a *person*."

"Did you still believe they were found in a cabbage patch? Oh, Muffin. I'm sorry to be the one to disillusion you."

"I don't know what I believed," he admitted, smirking at himself as he continued exploring the taut shape of her belly. "That babies were objects? A goal? Not..." The realization was creeping over him that he would have to shape this person the way he'd been shaped. There would be arguments and resistance and weariness. His own resentment at his responsibilities would be mirrored back to him and it would sting.

Even so, there was anticipation in him, too. He wanted to know what this new human would be like. Would they have Lexi's eyes and smile and guarded heart?

Her resistance to trusting him had been bothering him since she'd admitted to it. It told him exactly how much she'd been hurt in the past. And really, was it any wonder she didn't trust him to look after her? They were together one night and he had gotten her pregnant. Now he was crashing her life.

"I keep thinking I should apologize to you. Probably to the baby, too." He drew a slow circle with his palm, searching for another nudge.

"Oh, Gawd, I feel so selfish for making this baby have me as a mother." Her voice held laughter, but also distress. "Now there's this mountain of royal duties on top of it. Do you think they'll ever forgive us?"

"Maybe not. But I keep trying to regret that night and

I can't." He hadn't been interested in anyone else since her. The search for a "suitable" wife had only fed his sullenness. Now, however, a different fire was flickering to life within him.

It was passion. Obviously. He wanted this woman in ways that were very base and sexual. But there was another aspect he hesitated to examine. The darkness within him had become less dark the minute he'd had an excuse to fly across an ocean and confront her. To *see* her.

Now she was here in his bed, in his life. They had made a tiny being who would bind her to him forever. That pushed the darkness even further out, but at what cost?

He didn't let himself think of it, only slid closer and gathered her in, allowing his hand to run up her back beneath her shirt so he could mold her new shape to his front.

She stiffened in surprise, then gave a small shudder and relaxed. When he dipped his head to kiss her, she tucked her mouth into his chest.

"I haven't brushed my teeth."

"I don't care. Kiss me," he demanded.

He was in this strange headspace of tenderness and possessiveness and wanting to consume her. It took great effort to gentle his kiss when she let her head tip back. He reminded himself that her trust was tentative, that she was wary.

When she ran her hand into his loose hair, however, and pressed the back of his head while opening her mouth wider beneath his in hungry receptiveness, he abandoned restraint.

He crushed her mouth the way he'd been wanting to since he had glanced across a party in Monte Carlo and saw these pillowy lips part in shock. He slid his knee between hers and grabbed a handful of her lush ass and plundered her mouth with his tongue, trying to slake a thirst that had been driving him mad for months.

She moaned and ran her foot against his calf and slid her hand to the back of his neck, tongue sweeping out to find his.

The ample swell of her breast filled his hand, the silk and lace of her bra an erotic texture. He wanted what was beneath it—soft skin and the pebbled nipple. He swept his mouth down to gently bite through the layers of fabric, liking the way she gasped in pleasure.

"I was afraid you wouldn't find me sexy like this." Her hands were running over his shoulders and back, shifting his shirt against his skin as though she wanted to tear it off his body.

"What does this say about how sexy I think you are?" He moved so she could feel his erection against her thigh, then lifted his hips and opened his trousers, inviting her to caress him.

"This is just you waking up, isn't it?" She slid her hand into his loosened trousers and cupped his erection through his boxer briefs, dimming his ability to think.

"What about you? Are you waking up?" He worked his hands beneath the panel that was bunched beneath the roundness of her belly, finding the lace of her underwear.

She drew in a sharp breath, but she didn't stop him,

not even when he slid his hand around to her backside, pushing the trousers off her ass, down to her thighs so he could come back and trace the vee of silk that covered her mound.

"We, um…"

He liked how she'd lost her ability to speak. He slid a finger inside her panties and traced folds that were slippery and hot. *So* inviting.

Her mouth opened, but no sound came out, only the hiss of her breath. Her nails curled against shoulders and her breasts quivered.

"You said—" She bit her lip. Her eyelids fluttered. "Our seats?"

"We can circle the airport…" He let his fingertip roll around and around the engorged knot at the apex of her folds. "As long as you need."

She gave a small cry and pushed her face into his shoulder, but her hand found the top of his briefs and slipped inside. Her fist tightened around his erection as she slid her knee against his leg, opening her thighs for more of his touch.

"Let me kiss you again," he insisted.

She did. Passionately. They caressed each other as they feasted on each other, writhing and perspiring beneath the light blanket, gasping and moaning until she set her teeth in his bottom lip and groaned with ecstasy into his mouth.

As her hips bucked in orgasm, he let his own excitement take him over the edge, mindful of the fact they couldn't really stay in the air while he spent hours making love to her, even though this was exactly where he wanted to stay.

* * *

Lexi was still feeling undone when she took her seat.

She hadn't planned to fool around with Magnus. Her desire to see how he truly felt about the baby had turned into sexual desire and one thing led to another.

Discovering they still had a powerful physical connection wasn't as comforting as she'd imagined it would be. All she'd really learned was that she had even less willpower around him than she had believed.

The way he looked at her as she joined him, with lazy satisfaction and knowing possessiveness, only made her feel more at his mercy—of which he seemed to have very little.

Trying to avoid his gaze, she looked out the window where the sun cast golden beams across a collection of jagged islands, all wearing coats of emerald and ivory.

"Is that it?" She touched her forehead to the cool glass, studying the largest one. It was shaped like a bowl rimmed in granite teeth. A long, silvery-blue fjord stretched in a jagged wedge up the middle. The coastline was a cliff that had been broken off by the axe of an ancient ice age. In the distance, a half dozen smaller islands stood like weathered pyramids. "I expected it to be covered in snow."

"It's summer. And we're not as far north as people think. Also, the islands were formed by volcanoes, so we have enough thermal activity that the snow only sticks in the highest elevations."

"It's really pretty." She squashed her nose trying to keep it all in sight as they made their approach, growing more enchanted by the second. "Is that the palace?"

She pointed to a grouping of stone towers with spires and tile roofs. Stairs led from lawns to halls to terraced courtyards. A fat wall surrounded all of it.

"That's the original castle. One of Queen Katla's first acts was to name it a heritage site and return it along with its contents to Isleif. It's open to the public for guided tours. The palace is the long building behind it."

"Where you live."

"We. Yes."

We. He wasn't going to let up for a second, was he?

The palace wasn't as fairy-tale-looking, but she imagined it was modernized and far more comfortable than that magical-looking castle.

Seconds later, they touched down. Her nerves dissipated the way they always did when she was about to go on stage. It was a convenient Zen-like state that bordered on disassociation. It probably wasn't healthy, but it had gotten her through a lot of difficult times so she didn't fight it.

"Crowds have gathered," Ulmer informed as he brought Lexi a long coat. "Ignore them and move quickly into the car."

Lexi glanced at Magnus as she buttoned and belted the light coat that would disguise her pregnancy. "Do they know I'm here with you?"

"A video of us boarding is circulating online."

She had a quick look at her phone and saw herself climbing the stairs into the jet. Magnus's hand was splayed in her lower back, his wide shoulders shielding her as much as possible, but she'd been caught in a compromising profile.

Baby Bump or Booty Call? was trending, with comments ranging from *I knew it* and *#StanMagLexi* to *#golddigger* and worse. She clicked off her phone and dropped it into her pocket.

"Welcome to the cage, pretty bird," Magnus said flintily. He looped a scarf around her neck and set a woolen hat on her head.

"It's too big." She brushed the hat back before it slipped over her eyes. "I don't need this, do I?" He had just reminded her it was August.

"No, but I want you to wear them."

"Because they're Isleif colors?" She picked up the tail of the scarf, recognizing the stripes of blue and white and green.

"Because they're mine." He gave the edge of the hat a third roll against her forehead, smoothing her hair back from her cheeks as he did. "And so are you."

That should not have sent a frisson of pleasure through her, but it did.

"Sir?" Ulmer prompted as the door was opened and a fresh-scented gust of air came in, one that was sweet and cool and beckoning.

Outside, a cheer rose only to be abruptly cut off when the crowd realized it was only Ulmer. He was not the star they were waiting for.

Magnus took her hand and drew her out the door where he paused on the top step, holding her firmly in the loop of his arm as he casually waved.

"I thought—" Lexi noted that Ulmer was glaring at them from the bottom of the steps.

"Wave." Magnus leaned down to speak next to her

ear. "They love shots like this, that look like I had something to say that was so urgent and personal it couldn't wait."

"Something that implies we have private jokes?" She cupped his bearded cheek so she could look into his eyes with her most captivated expression. "Something that says, *I've never been so enamored with anyone in my life*?"

"Damn." His pupils flared. "You're good at this."

"I know." She smiled her cheekiest smile and gave the crowd a wave that caused them to roar. Then she and Magnus descended the stairs without hurry and climbed into the waiting car.

The windows were tinted and they had a police escort to allow them to exceed speed limits, not stopping for lights, but the road was lined with spectators, many waving Isleif flags.

"I feel like they don't…hate me?" she suggested tentatively.

"We've worked very hard to ensure the prince maintains a high approval rating," Ulmer said stiffly, attention on his tablet. "Weddings and babies are always popular. We're hoping that news will counter any negative attention that arises from y—"

"Ulmer," Magnus cut in, quiet and lethal. "We're not going to play the blame game. We're especially not going to make Lexi pay for my decisions."

"No, sir. Of course not," Ulmer said promptly, nodding contritely at her.

Ulmer and I play a game of tit for tat, but he won't be able to retaliate with you. I won't allow it.

"Ulmer?" Lexi bit her lip. Magnus could say he wouldn't tolerate pettiness against her, but she knew exactly how cold wars and passive-aggressiveness worked. She didn't want to be subjected to it if she could avoid it. "If you tell me what you need, I will stay on script and hit my mark every single time."

"I appreciate that, Ms. Alexander. Thank you." Ulmer sounded sincere, then looked to his tablet and added under his breath. "I can't tell you how refreshing that would be."

Lexi was given an hour to freshen up before meeting the queen.

Nothing like this had been in her plans so she was provided a small wardrobe from which she chose a three-quarter-length stony-green wrap dress. It was demure yet flattering and made by a local designer. Her hair went up in a simple chignon and she applied her own makeup in natural colors.

Before she could decide on jewelry, Magnus returned from wherever he'd gone. He held a gold coin dangling from a thick gold chain.

"It's an old custom to offer a woman a coin as a promise, usually when a man was leaving for a raid, in case he didn't return, especially if she had someone to provide for."

"It's pretty." She caught the coin to study it. It wasn't big, but it was surprisingly heavy, telling her it was solid gold. "Are you going somewhere?"

"After pulling this stunt? The dungeon, I imagine." He twirled his finger.

She turned so he could affix the chain around her neck. While he was there, he kissed her nape, sending a shiver down her spine.

"Thank you for the plane." His warm breath wafted against her skin as he nuzzled behind her ear. "I didn't get a chance to say that."

"Don't—" She blushed so hard her cheeks stung.

"Now you won't be so nervous." There was an amused glint in his eyes. He knew exactly what he had done to her.

"You're a menace," she muttered as she took the arm he offered her.

Ansgar Palace was as modern as a two-hundred-year-old building could be. It was full of historic art and odd echoes and staff who moved like ghosts, glimpsed briefly before they disappeared, leaving her to wonder if she'd actually seen them.

Not that Lexi was taking much of it in. She was more preoccupied with wondering if she could enlist the queen in delaying her marriage to Magnus.

Just when Lexi was about to ask *Are we there yet?* they arrived at a door with a guard outside it. Magnus rang a doorbell and a butler—footman?—let them into a formal receiving room, offering a deferential bow as he did.

Lexi barely got her bearings with a quick scan of a desk, a fireplace and a grouping of elegant furniture before Queen Katla demanded her attention without saying a word.

The queen was a handsome woman in a forest green dress. Her hair was pulled back from her face with pearl-studded combs, revealing tasteful chandelier earrings. She remained seated, expression dispassionate.

Lexi tightened her fist into Magnus's sleeve as he performed the introduction.

Lexi curtsied, murmuring, "It's an honor to meet you, Your Majesty."

"Sorr requires you," Queen Katla said to Magnus. "He's in his study."

"I'll stop in when we get back to that end of the palace."

"It's important."

"I doubt it."

A silent battle of wills waged between their locked stare.

"You forced my hand when you came off the plane," the queen said with muted fury. "You know you did. *Go*."

Magnus looked to Lexi. His cheek ticked.

Her heart began battering inside her rib cage. She had thought Magnus was defying *Ulmer* when they'd waved from the plane, but he'd been playing power games with his sister.

"I would never leave you anywhere that you would be unsafe," he said, making her heart swerve. "I'll be back in fifteen minutes."

As she was left alone with the queen, Lexi drew a subtle, shaken breath, hoping she could believe him, but she couldn't help wondering if there really was a dungeon here, and whether his sister had the desire to consign her to it.

"Sit," Katla ordered with a nod at a nearby chair. It

didn't look nearly as comfortable or ornate as her own. "Has Magnus explained that I've endured enough scandal and heartache for a dozen lifetimes, Alexandra?"

"Please call me Lexi. If you want to," she added weakly, swallowing under Katla's glare at being interrupted.

"My mother died from an undiagnosed heart defect when I was ten. My brother died by suicide a few years later. It's too easy to say that losing our mother made him give up hope. Our father was the more likely reason. He was not an easy man even when she was alive. He grew more demanding and intractable as time went on. I kept as many of his scandals behind palace walls as I could, but there was enough in the public record for six hours of a salacious, unauthorized documentary. His assassination was not unexpected, considering how many people he had crossed in his lifetime. I've since dedicated my life to righting his wrongs."

Lexi didn't move, didn't say anything. She barely dared breathe.

"Every decision, every sacrifice I have made, has been justified by my love for Isleif. I married a man I barely knew because he had the intelligence to create opportunity and prosperity for our people. Sorr has the heart of a good father, too. I saw my marriage as a means to build a better country and thus a better world to leave to my children. I very arrogantly believed I would produce a better ruler, too."

Ah. Here was the point she was making.

"I've never been able to conceive."

"Magnus said. I'm very sorry." Lexi self-consciously

slid her hands off her bump and into what should have been her lap.

"It's not your fault, but I'll admit to being sick with envy. One and done? It's so unfair it's beyond cruel. I've learned to ignore such things because I still have the power to leave a better ruler, Alexandra."

Magnus. Everything within Lexi stilled.

"I know I'm not an ideal partner for him," Lexi said haltingly, seeing her chance. "That's why I've asked him to wait on marriage."

Katla snorted. "But you can see how he boxed us in by waving from the plane. He drives me mad at times, finding ways to get around me, but I can't complain about how shrewd and combative he is about getting his way. He needs qualities like that to rule well."

"What he doesn't need is a woman who drags him into the trash with her," Lexi acknowledged.

"Exactly."

Ouch. Lexi couldn't go back and change all the decisions in her life, though. Far too many had been made for her, leading up to this checkered history that followed her. She couldn't look at the queen. Her eyes were too hot, her humility too bone-deep. She willed the door to open and for Magnus to come in and save her, even though she doubted she would ever escape this sense of being judged unworthy.

"Magnus has made it clear that you are the wife he wants," Katla said quietly. "I *have* to believe he knows what he is doing. That somehow, this union will benefit not just him, but Isleif."

And the world? Lexi strangled a hysterical laugh. *No pressure.*

"I hope you'll use this chance to reset your image. Keep both of you out of the trash."

It was a harsh thing to say, but it also awakened Lexi to the possibility that this *was* a chance to reinvent herself. Marrying Magnus could be more than playing the part of someone "better." She could do better. *Be* better.

"I want to be someone my child can be proud of." The admission came from the depths of her dented soul, where she secretly wondered if she *deserved* for people to use her for their own ends. "I would like to be someone that Magnus, and Isleif, could be proud of. I hope…" She had to clear a thickness from her throat. "I hope you'll provide guidance when necessary?"

"I'm not shy with my opinions. Lexi."

Was that— It was sarcasm, but the friendly kind. A tiny glow of optimism flickered to life inside her.

The door thrust inward, making Lexi jump in surprise.

Magnus strode in on his own momentum, throwing the door closed behind him with another bang that made her stiffen and widen her eyes at him.

"Eleven minutes. Did you run?" Katla said with a sniff. "You didn't even give yourself time to choose properly."

"I knew which one I wanted as soon as I saw it." He showed the ring pinched between his finger and thumb. "The emerald matches her eyes."

"I've always liked that one." The queen nodded approval. "It belonged to our great-grandmother. A gift from a Russian czar."

Lexi was speechless as Magnus picked up her hand. She wanted to remind him that she hadn't yet agreed to marry him, but he slid the ring onto her finger so quickly, she was only able to admire it once it was there.

It was gorgeous, with a green stone flanked by three white diamonds on either side in a gold setting of old-world craftsmanship.

"It's beautiful." Heavy.

This is a chance, she kept hearing Katla said. *A chance.*

But was she really up to the task? Because this wasn't a role. It was a position, one she couldn't leave once she took it.

Their engagement would give her time to think about it, though, so she pushed the ring a little more firmly onto her finger.

"When is the baby due?" Katla asked. "I'd like you married before it arrives."

"I told Ulmer to arrange it for Thursday," Magnus said.

"What?" Lexi gasped, very afraid she was about to faint again.

CHAPTER NINE

"FINALLY," MAGNUS SAID when Lexi walked out of her bedroom in a robe and slippers the following morning.

After a long, stilted dinner with Katla and Sorr, she'd left Magnus with a few cross words about things moving too fast and locked herself in her room to call her mother. He'd peeked in on her a few hours later, finding her fast asleep, so he'd left her to sleep alone.

Twelve hours later, he was concerned enough that he'd canceled a morning meeting. He set aside the report he was reading and rose to press the backs of his fingers against her cheeks and forehead. She was warm, but not too warm. Pink, but not flushed or glassy-eyed.

"I was about to put a mirror under your nose. Are you ill?"

"Yesterday was a lot." She blinked foggily. "So is assembling a baby." She sent a startled look to the servants who bustled in to reset the breakfast table for her. "It's only nine thirty, isn't it?"

"Yes, but we have a lunch engagement."

"Thank you." She smiled as a young woman set a dish of yogurt and berries in front of her. "Should I skip ordering eggs? What time is lunch? Will it be here?"

"Late. At the cottage." He nodded for the eggs.

"What cottage?" Lexi asked.

"My mother's. The one where she grew up. When I called to ask her to come for the wedding, she wanted to meet you right away so I had them flown in this morning."

"Them?"

"My sister and her family live with her. The house in Bergen is very big." Magnus had provided it once he had access to palace funds, so his mother would have the privacy she deserved. "I usually visit her there, but she still has her parents' cottage here. She's staying until the wedding."

"Magnus—"

"You need to meet her regardless, Lexi."

Lexi paused with her spoonful of berries halfway to her mouth. "I guess this is her grandchild, isn't it? Her first? No, you just said your sister has children."

"Two, yes. She's still on maternity leave with the second."

"What about your brother? Will he be there?"

"I don't know."

Lexi delved for more, but he looked away, signaling for a coffee he didn't want, loath to explain that the last time he'd seen Freyr had been his brother's wedding, but it had been strained by the fact that Sveyn had been there. They hadn't had much contact since.

Magnus couldn't seem to talk *to* his siblings. How was he supposed to talk about them? He turned to a more pleasant topic.

"We should discuss our honeymoon, since security

will have to prescreen the location. I can only clear one week. Do you have any thoughts on where you'd like to spend it?"

"Seriously?" she asked snippily. "I've told you I'm not ready to marry you and, frankly, the only place I'm eager to go is back to bed—" She winced and covered her eyes. "I mean..."

"Oh, no." He chuckled, enjoying this. "You can't back out now. You said it so that's where we'll spend it. I'll tell Ulmer to keep a chiropractor on standby."

"Stop it," she said firmly, still blushing. "I'm saying I'm not interested in more travel. And if we don't get married, we don't need a honeymoon." She poked her tongue out at him!

They were getting married. He drew the line at bullying her into it, but he'd find a way to convince her.

In the meanwhile, he quietly told Ulmer they would honeymoon at the health spa on one of the smaller islands. It was a pretty location with natural pools of different temperatures. At least two of them were touted as beneficial in pregnancy so he knew it would be safe for her.

Whatever lightness had come into his mood while contemplating his honeymoon had dissipated by the time they left for the cottage.

The palace was situated on the south side of the mouth of the fjord. The cottage was all the way on the north side, but they took the ferry, which cut forty minutes off the drive.

Forty minutes that Magnus could have used to brood.

Family visits shouldn't be this oppressive! In many

ways they were no different from other appearances. Dress up, show up, shake hands, listen politely, pose for a photo if asked.

They weren't even strangers. Well. They were to some extent, he supposed. He had a standing appointment in his calendar to call his mother and made a point of seeing her a few times a year, typically around birthdays or holidays. He had attended his siblings' weddings and texted appropriate felicitations on other life events when prompted by Ulmer, but he was no longer close with them.

Today, that felt more significant than usual. He wasn't sure why. He wasn't worried that his mother would say something to upset Lexi or the other way around. He wasn't embarrassed by his roots, either.

His visits with family were always prickly, though. Rather than address things, they swept them under the rug, but they were still there—his mother's pain, his father's abandonment, Magnus's abrupt departure to Isleif and his sense of being cut off from his brother and sister against his will.

Yes, he did feel blamed for it, even though it was merely the hand he'd been dealt.

He had a feeling Lexi would navigate all of it without any problem, though. She was a people-pleaser, barely in the palace twenty-four hours and the staff was already charmed by her.

Something about introducing her to his family grated on him, though. Some of it was possessiveness, he acknowledged. They were new and she was his. He wasn't ready to share her, but there was more to it.

A latent fear that she would take sides, perhaps? Take *their* side?

"Are we here?" Lexi had been watching out the window with great interest and now sat up taller as they turned into the long drive. "How does she keep sheep if she doesn't live here?"

"She sharecrops with a neighbor and lets the house for vacation rentals. Security has gone through here. Don't worry."

"I can honestly say I've never felt so safe as when I'm with you," she said wryly.

That remark should have pleased him. It did, before the SUV rolled to a stop outside the stone cottage and an unexpected threat emerged with the rest of the people pouring out the front door.

First was his mother, Truda, with her white-blond hair coming out of its knot and her smile faltering as she shaded her eyes. His four-year-old niece was next. She jumped up and down and waved madly.

His sister, Dalla, hurried out to set her hand on the little girl's shoulder, trying to keep her feet on the ground. Dalla's husband came out with a swaddled infant against his shoulder. Then Magnus's brother Freyr and his redheaded wife. She looked almost as pregnant as Lexi.

Last was a man who had a lot more gray in his beard than he'd had when Magnus had spotted him at Freyr's wedding two years ago.

"Why the *hell* wasn't I advised he was here?" Magnus barked. And why was he looping his arm around Truda?

"He was on the list, sir." The bodyguard in the passenger seat took out his phone. "I understood it had been forwarded to you—"

"Oh, for God's sake. It doesn't matter now, does it?"

"Who—?" Lexi asked warily.

"My father. Sveyn."

As far as Lexi was concerned, it was a pleasant afternoon. Everyone was polite and friendly if careful not to overstep. The women had a lot of questions about her pregnancy and how Lexi and Magnus had met. The men asked if she knew this or that action star. The food was excellent and the children were adorable.

In many ways, they were the kind of close-knit family Lexi had always longed for, with their cheeky asides and small digressions into each other's lives.

It would have been a perfect day if Magnus hadn't been such a looming presence through it all, speaking very little, creating a tension that was so thick, it could have been spooned into bowls like porridge.

At one point, while Lexi was in the washroom, she heard a few sharp words in Isleifisch. When she came back, the room went silent. Everyone wore stiff expressions. Sveyn had left the room.

"Would you like to walk with me to the beach?" Lexi asked Magnus's niece, even though the little girl didn't speak English. It was a windy day, but Magnus had warned Lexi that they might walk so she'd worn short boots, wool trousers and a cowl-necked sweater with a short coat.

Dalla came with them. Lexi could see her trying to

engage Magnus, trying to repair whatever disagreement had happened in those few minutes Lexi had been absent.

Lexi deliberately lagged behind them to study a tide pool, pointing to interest the little girl, trying to give Dalla a minute alone with Magnus, but he only stopped and waited for her, expression stoic.

When they got back to the cottage, Truda tried to speak to Magnus alone, but he insisted they had commitments at the palace to get back to.

Looking teary, Truda hugged Lexi and said, "I know you're both very busy, but we'll be here all week. Come by anytime. Anytime."

"Thank you. It was so lovely to meet you all." Lexi said a warm goodbye, aware of Magnus only offering stiff nods.

He said nothing on the way back to the palace and they were both tied up for a few hours once they returned. She didn't know what mysterious meetings he had, but she was met by a stylist and her team of seamstresses who were assembling a wardrobe of maternity fashions to give Lexi an appropriate selection through the rest of her pregnancy.

The woman had a handful of wedding gowns for Lexi to try on, too.

Mindful of the fact the woman was only doing her job, Lexi went along with choosing one, but after their visit with his family, she had more doubts than ever about rushing into marriage to Magnus. If things didn't work out between them, would she wind up sitting in a room full of undercurrents like today? She wasn't sure if he was holding a grudge or what, but it had been very uncomfortable.

She was exhausted when she finished with the stylist, but she went looking for Magnus, determined to take a stand on the wedding before this runaway train arrived at the altar.

Their apartment took up two corners in this wing of the palace and his bedroom was suitably grand with a massive fireplace, a sitting area, a desk and a bed the size of an ice rink. He was seated in a wingback chair, a glass of something amber in his hand.

"Do I have to dress for dinner tonight?" she asked after he invited her to enter.

"It's just us. It's in the schedule," he said stonily.

She knew. She'd used the question as an excuse to come in here. Now she pressed the door closed behind her.

"Can we talk?" she asked.

"Not about my family," he clarified into his glass.

"About the wedding."

He gulped, then hissed out a breath. "My mother asked if my father could come as her date. They've reconciled."

"Oh." She didn't know what surprised her more. That statement or the fact that he was sharing it on the heels of insisting he didn't want to talk about his family. She came forward to perch in the chair that sat at an angle to his. "Did you tell her you'd rather not?"

"I said I didn't care. They're adults. They can do what they want." He took another hefty gulp.

She studied him, trying to read more in his expression than he was saying aloud, but he was very good at hiding his thoughts and feelings.

"It must have been a shock for him to learn his wife had had an affair, even though it was before they were married."

"It wasn't an affair," he said darkly.

"A—" *A hookup like us?* That was what she almost said, but her heart twisted in her chest as understanding dawned. Magnus wasn't sulking or holding a grudge. He was hurting. "Oh, Magnus."

He only curled his lip and sipped.

"Did the queen know?"

"Yes. She helped my mother leave the palace the night she was assaulted, then paid her to keep quiet. Or, I should say, she offered a settlement that my mother agreed was fair," he said pithily, as though quoting something he'd been told but didn't buy. "Once my father— Sveyn—realized it hadn't been consensual, he wanted the truth to come out, but my mother wouldn't hear of it."

"It's her story." Lexi had had her own run-ins with handsy men over the years. It had never been as grave as what his mother had suffered, but she preferred to put those experiences as far behind her as possible, not revisit them. She completely understood Truda's desire to forget.

"My father couldn't see past his anger at the palace. Once I agreed to live here, I became one of them. The enemy."

"That's horrible. But his reaction is not your fault, Magnus."

"Don't psychoanalyze me." He flashed an icy glance

at her. "I knew what I was doing when I agreed to come. More or less. I mean, I didn't want any of this, but Katla is very persuasive. She suspected from the time I was born that I was her brother. She said she *gave* me that time with my family. And that if she'd had her own children, she wouldn't have prevailed on me, but I was being called. What kind of man was I, at my core? The kind who knows he's needed and walks away?"

"That was a lot to put on you when you were barely a man." The words hit her like a ton of bricks. She could only imagine how they had landed on him.

"I thought my father would eventually see my side of it, that I didn't really have a choice, but he wouldn't talk to me. He didn't talk to any of us for a good year, not until he divorced my mother. Then he insisted on shared custody of Dalla and Freyr, driving us further apart."

"He turned them against you?"

"Maybe it would have happened anyway. I couldn't see much of any of them. I was here and they were still in Norway, but I speak to my mother every month. She never mentioned that she'd been seeing him since Freyr's wedding *two years ago*. He's been living at the house I bought her for *four months*."

"And this is the first you're hearing of it?"

"Yes."

"And it feels like another secret that was kept from you."

"That's exactly what it is." He drained the last of his drink and clacked the empty glass onto the side table.

She left her chair and slid into his lap.

He stiffened. "I don't want pity."

"It's comfort." She draped her legs over the armrest, ignoring his scowl. "That was very insensitive of them."

"I don't expect them to be sensitive," he muttered as his arm curved behind her back in a way that seemed more reactive than conscious. His other hand found her hip so he could pull her more snugly into him. "I expect them to be honest."

"Then be honest with me. You weren't happy about our going to see them even before we saw Sveyn was there. Why?"

"I don't know." He sounded irritated. "I knew they would like you and they did."

"I liked them."

"I knew you would." He hesitated, then he continued in a very low voice. "I knew you would have a place with them, that they would welcome you like you're one of them. But I don't have a place with them anymore. I didn't want to watch you go where I couldn't."

Oh, Magnus.

She tucked the side of her face into the hollow of his shoulder and cupped the silky whiskers on his jaw.

He caught her hand and drew it down, but held on to it.

"I feel like a ghost when I'm with them. I watch them get on with their lives without me. Now even my father is back in the picture."

And it hurt him so much, he could hardly speak of it.

"I think they love you and don't know how to reach you," she said, thinking of the way they'd looked to Lexi to be that conduit, asking her questions that Magnus never would have answered.

"Because I'm *here*. And what the hell am I supposed to do about that?" he asked.

She didn't know, but she felt for his family, unable to scale the real and invisible walls that surrounded him. She had a suspicion he'd just told her more about his feelings for his family than he'd consciously clarified to himself before. And, if he was anything like her, he was about to pull back inside his protective walls and shut her out, rather than stay in a state of exposure.

But she was *here*. And this was the kind of intimacy she longed for between them. The kind that gave her hope and the confidence to reach out to him in a way they both could accept. A way that would reinforce these delicate emotional bridges.

She curled into him, lifting so she could set her mouth into the crook of his neck while she slid her hand up his arm to his chest, where she touched one of the buttons on his shirt.

His hold on her changed. He looked down with eyes narrowed in suspicion. "Still comfort?"

"Opportunity," she said lightly. "Unless you'd rather wait until after dinner?" She pretended to try leaving his lap.

"No." He gathered her as he stood and carried her to the bed.

"Lexi." Magnus brushed the hair off her neck and buried his lips against the spot that made her shiver and gasp. "You have to get up and get dressed."

"No," she grumbled, scowling at the daylight pouring through the open curtains, then glanced over her shoulder to see him sprawled on the bed behind her, fully dressed. "Why are you up already?"

"Because your mother is landing soon."

"Magnus." She rolled onto her back to glare at him.

He lifted onto his elbow. "I told you I was having her flown in for the wedding. Are you going to tell me you wanted your brother and sister here after all?"

"No. They're out of my life. But *I* told *you* that I'm not prepared to marry you in some rush-to-the-altar, shotgun wedding."

His expression cooled. "Was there something in the prenup that you didn't like?"

He had forwarded the documents after dinner last night, when she'd still been floating in the afterglow of their lovemaking. Then he'd left for a conference call.

Annoyed, she had nearly deleted them unread, but she never considered a role without reading the fine print of the offer so she had begrudgingly pored through them.

Despite seeming very fair, they had put her to sleep. He had come to bed later, not disturbing her beyond a spoon and a kiss, so they hadn't talked about the wedding and now her mother was here, expecting to see her daughter married.

"The terms are fine." She sat up. "It's the unreasonable demands of the director that are putting me off. You can't just book a wedding and order me to show up for it, Magnus. That's not how it works."

"Have you been paying attention at all?" He swung his legs off the bed and sat there a moment with his back to her.

She saw his fist clench before he smoothed his hand

open and rubbed it on his thigh. Then he drew a breath and stood to look down on her.

"I will be at our wedding the day after tomorrow. Whether you join me at the altar depends on what kind of woman you are, doesn't it? What are you afraid of? That this life might be hard? It will be. Life is hard. This life, here in the palace, can be very hard. It is lonely and it is bigger than either of us, but you are carrying the next person who will shoulder this burden, Lexi. What are you going to tell them? That you didn't marry their father because you didn't have the guts for it? Fine. If that's true then you're right. You're not fit to wear my ring or a crown. I have places to be."

He walked out, pulling the door closed firmly behind him.

Lexi refused to cry, but she was still upset when she collected her mother from her guest room and brought her to the suite she shared with Magnus.

"I *knew* you did more than dance with him," Rhonda said the second they were alone. She wasn't looking at her, though. She was taking in the decor of rare art and hand-loomed carpets and luxurious furnishings. "I thought our room was nice. Did he make you sign a prenup?"

"Mom."

"What? Don't be stupid, Lexi. I presume he's making you give up your career. You'd better protect yourself."

Rhonda wasn't a bad person, merely ambitious. If an opportunity presented, she wanted a piece of it. And having watched the spikes and dips in Lexi's career, she knew things could change in a blink.

Always keep something for a rainy day was her motto.

"Are you?" Rhonda asked. "Giving up acting?"

"I've spoken to Bernadette," Lexi admitted reluctantly. "I told her I should be able to keep my funding in place, but that I can't commit to the role." Lexi had plenty to invest now. Magnus was covering her expenses and the prenup left all her previous assets in her own hands. Plus, it made arrangements for her support moving forward. It was actually very generous, not that she told her mother any of that.

"You're not sleeping." Rhonda spied the shadows beneath Lexi's eyes despite the cover-up she'd applied. "Nerves? It's one day. One performance."

Is that all this wedding was? Why was she agonizing then?

The performance part of it didn't bother her, even though the "family only" guest list had bloated to over a hundred and fifty dignitaries from Isleif and neighboring countries. The ceremony was being broadcast internationally and a parade was planned so the people of Isleif could glimpse their future queen in the flesh.

But that was Rhonda. *It doesn't matter if you're running a fever. The show must go on.*

"This is a lot of power, though," her mother mused as she cast another concerned look at the mural on the ceiling and the hand-carved molding and the portrait of the queen on the wall. "What if you decide to leave? What if they decide they don't want you here?"

"Magnus wouldn't throw me out. He wouldn't do that to our baby." She felt confident in that, at least. He had made it clear that he wanted their baby to know both its parents and he had confided how cut off he felt from his own family. "If he wanted to get rid of me, he wouldn't be marrying me."

"Or he's cementing his position."

"*Mom.* Don't be so cynical."

"You know better than to be naive about something like this. What happens to the baby if you divorce him?"

"The baby grows up here. It's their heritage. I respect that." She did. And she understood that meant her baby would always be here so she should be here, too.

What would happen if she didn't marry Magnus? Would he marry someone else who would not only be his queen, but would have influence over their child's life? *No.* That didn't sit well with her at all.

She didn't get a chance to talk privately to Magnus again. She saw him at dinner, but it was a small but formal thing with her mother, the queen, and a handful of royalty who were visiting for the wedding. The day before the wedding, Lexi entertained those wives while Magnus was in talks with their husbands. Queen Claudia, the one Lexi had been so awestruck by in Paris, along with Queen Cassiopeia—"call me Sopi"—and Princess Amy of Vallia were all delightfully down-to-earth, which reassured her that maybe she could rise to the station Magnus was offering her.

If he was still offering it. He'd been very cold yesterday. *I will be at our wedding*, he had said. But would he?

After such a busy day, she couldn't keep her eyes open and fell asleep before Magnus got back to their suite. Suddenly, she was waking to a light breakfast and more fussing than any red carpet she'd ever walked.

Her mother did her makeup and praised the A-line gown as "perfection" with its lace sleeves and chiffon overlay on the skirt. Queen Katla had provided a tiara to hold the veil and Magnus had gifted her beautiful teardrop diamonds for her ears.

When it came to the ceremony itself, Lexi hadn't weighed in much. She'd been letting Magnus make all the decisions while she had stubbornly sat on the fence. As a result, he'd chosen a traditional vein and she was told that most of it would be performed in Isleifisch.

At the last second, she sent him a note with a request.

She didn't receive a response. She was only told that he'd seen it.

They arrived at the chapel and Lexi was an uncharacteristic mass of nerves. It was worse than any stage fright she'd ever experienced, but it had nothing to do with the crowds or the unfamiliar words or the huge step she was taking.

Would he do as she'd asked? It felt hugely important that he make this one small concession. Would he?

The music began and his niece led the procession of bridesmaids out the door. Prince Sorr was supposed to escort her down the aisle. She could have asked her mother, but Lexi had grown up as something that her mother lent out. She didn't want to be "given away" by anyone. She didn't want to become something that Magnus acquired.

So Prince Sorr was already at the front of the chapel next to the queen. Lexi was forced to take on faith that her future husband understood her at least a little and would be waiting to walk down the aisle *with* her.

She stepped out of the anteroom, breath held, and there he was, acutely handsome in a green military-style jacket with blue cuffs and collar. It had gold epaulets and he wore his sash with various medals and other regalia. The hilt of a long sword sat against his hip.

He wore his long hair smoothed into its customary gather. His beard was freshly shaped. He held out his gloved hands and she went toward him without hesitation.

"I knew you wouldn't disappoint me." His rasped words and the glow of pride in his gaze brought tears to her eyes. "You were made for this, goddess. You were made to be mine."

Was marrying him a huge mistake? In this moment, it felt like the best and only decision she could make. She took his arm and walked down the aisle with him, feeling as though they were giving themselves to each other. It felt *right*.

When she spoke her vows, she did so with care, clearly and firmly even as her chest was filled with butterflies. They exchanged rings and were pronounced married and he lifted her veil.

Everything fell away—the pomp and the crowd

and even the baby swelling her middle. In that eternal space between heartbeats, they were simply a man and a woman, pledging their lives to each other. He pressed his mouth to hers and it was done.

CHAPTER TEN

THEY DID SPEND much of their honeymoon in bed. At least, Lexi did. Magnus had always been a high-energy person so he went a little stir-crazy.

He swam a lot of laps while Lexi snoozed in their room at the spa, but it turned out to be a good choice. It was exclusive enough that the privacy expectations were already high. They mingled among the other guests and everyone was very respectful, but Lexi could only go in the cooler pools and she was never in them long anyway.

They made love a lot, usually with her on top which drove Magnus crazy in the best possible way. He wanted her to be comfortable and he wanted to be gentle, which meant it was slow and lazy and so delicious he nearly passed out from erotic joy.

They returned to the news that she had developed a small blood sugar issue. It wasn't severe enough to alarm the doctors, but they were adjusting her diet and were agreeing with Magnus's prediction that the baby would be big.

What the hell was it with people who wanted to touch her belly, though? After their honeymoon, they attended their first official function at a summit in Brussels. They were at a dinner and, in the middle of introducing her to an ambassador, the man bracketed her belly with both his hands as if he had every right to touch her!

Magnus nearly caused an international incident.

Lexi confided afterward that it wasn't the first time. "The irony is, I thought being married and very pregnant would put a stop to the groping. Joke's on me."

Magnus instructed their bodyguards to step in if he wasn't there to do it himself, but she only attended two more events before she begged to stay home.

She was still three weeks from her due date, but Magnus had an important presentation to offer at a climate conference in Dubai. He would only be gone a few days, but he was reluctant to leave her.

Her physician assured him everything was fine: her blood pressure was good, her glucose levels were under control, and her iron was exactly where it should be.

"If her body is telling her to rest then she should listen to it," the doctor said. "She might be experiencing an urge to nest, which could account for her desire to stay home. That's very normal, too."

Nest? They had staff to scrub baseboards and set up the nursery, but if she wanted to refold all the towels, he supposed he should get out of her way.

He left the following morning, but he was immediately discontent. Dubai was hot and dry and going back to his suite after his first meeting annoyed him. The rooms weren't empty. They were never empty. He was never alone, but the place *felt* empty. He much preferred when he could walk into a room and find Lexi reading a book or doing her stretches. She would tell him why the book she was reading would make a good movie or ask his opinion on the list of names she was compiling. He would rub her feet and that would turn into fooling around. And even though she was up constantly through the night, disturbing him every time, he preferred to sleep with her than have the bed to himself.

He missed her. There. He had admitted it.

Now what? he thought with disgust.

He was accepting his second cup of coffee the following morning, glancing over the notes for his presentation, when she called him.

He frowned. It was only 4:00 a.m. at home.

"It's early," he said in lieu of a greeting. "Are you all right?"

"I think I'm in labor."

"Also early." That's why he'd been persuaded to keep this commitment. The guideline was that she could deliver two weeks on either side of her due date, but that window didn't open for another week. "Have you spoken to the doctor?"

"No."

"Why not?"

"Because I wasn't sure if that's what it was. Besides, what can he do about it?"

"Help you prepare to deliver the baby?" Magnus suggested. He snapped his fingers at Ulmer. "Lexi thinks she's in labor. Get hold of the palace and—"

Ulmer was already nodding and walking away with his own phone pressed to his ear.

"The doctor will be there shortly," Magnus assured her. "How long have you been having contractions?"

"On and off all night. They kept going away so I kept trying to go back to sleep. My water hasn't broken and it's not that bad—" She drew a small breath.

"Is that a pain? Ulmer!" he shouted.

"The physician is on his way to her room," Ulmer said, peeking around the door. "I'm speaking to the pilot."

"I don't want to have the baby if you're not here," Lexi's small voice said in his ear.

"Is that why you didn't call the doctor? Lex, I don't want that, either, but I don't think that's up to us. If it happens, it happens."

"I know, but..." She took a shaken breath that almost sounded as though she was fighting tears. "It's fine. I'll figure it out."

He suddenly recalled her saying *Everyone I've ever known has let me down.*

"Lex, I'm leaving right now," Magnus told her, impatiently waving at Ulmer who was trying to direct staff to pack. He didn't need his damned toothbrush! "I'll be home before—" He couldn't lie to her, much as he wanted to. "Before dinner."

Would the baby arrive by then? Would she have to deliver alone?

"I'm sorry," she murmured.

"Don't be sorry. I shouldn't have left."

"But that presentation—"

"Will be given by someone else. I'll see you soon." He kept the phone to his ear while Ulmer helped him with his jacket.

There was a long space of dead air, the kind that another couple would have filled with words like *I love you*.

That infernal buzz, the one that warned him of an upheaval arriving in his life, started to coalesce, but it was cut off as she spoke.

"I think the doctor is here."

"Can you get up to let him in or—"

"He came in. Hi. I'm sorry to bother you," he heard her say before she added, "Bye, Magnus."

"I'll be there soon," he promised, but she had ended the call.

He received updates every hour. She was definitely in labor. A midwife was staying with her and keeping her comfortable. Katla checked on her, but things were progressing slowly. Lexi's water broke so she had a shower. She was taken to the hospital.

It was excruciating and he wasn't the one in labor!

Finally, the plane landed and they sped through the streets to get to the hospital. Magnus hurried to the maternity wing where the palace physician gave him a worried look.

"Her labor isn't progressing. She's been stuck at three centimeters since she arrived. We're monitoring the fetus for stress. The baby is fine, but I'm concerned about the princess. She's hasn't accepted any pain relief, only the TENS and she abandoned it because it wasn't helping. She hasn't slept or eaten since last night."

"Then feed her."

"But if surgery becomes necessary—"

"Why would she need that?" he asked with alarm.

"The baby is larger than average. She would have

struggled regardless, but when it comes time to push, I'm not sure she'll have the strength, now that she's distressed and exhausted."

"Let me talk to her."

Magnus walked into a darkened room that was a little too warm for comfort. Lexi wore a cotton nightgown rucked up to her thighs. She sat on an oversize ball, leaning forward, keening softly. The midwife sat in a chair before her, offering her arms to stabilize her.

"Lex, I'm here," he said softly.

He waited until Lexi quieted and started to sit up. Then he jerked his head to dismiss the midwife and took the seat. He cupped Lexi's elbows and set his feet on either side of the ball to keep it steady.

"What time is it?" she asked distractedly.

"They said you're not taking anything for the pain? Why not?"

"Because I need to stay sober, so I know what's going on." She clamped her hands around his forearms and winced. "These things are constant. Why aren't they *working*?"

She keened softly again, for a solid minute.

He waited, breath backed up in his lungs until she relaxed and panted.

"We talked about pain relief in birthing class. Remember? Let them give you something."

"I just told you." She squeezed his arms so hard it pinched. "They'll make me sick or stupid. I won't be able to walk. Walking is supposed to— *Argh!*"

Her cry was as much frustration as pain and it cut through him like a knife.

"Lexi." He tried to smooth her hair from falling over her eye, but she knocked his hand away. "Listen to me," he insisted. "They're worried. They want you to agree to surgery."

"They said the baby is fine." She touched the belt on her bump and snapped a look to the monitor.

"*You* are not. You're exhausted. You didn't sleep last night. You can't keep on like this."

"You don't know what I can do!" she cried. "You sure as hell aren't going to do it, are you? I have to do this myself. Oh my God." She folded forward.

He caught her before her knees hit the floor and gathered her into his lap. Her fist pressed into his shoulder in resistance even as she muffled her moan of agony in his chest.

"I don't know what to do," she said piteously, shoulders shuddering. "What if the baby needs me? I'll be unconscious. What if... I can't give up, Magnus?"

Give up control, she meant. She couldn't trust that she would be taken care of. That their baby would be.

"Lexi...*søta.*" The endearment was one his father had used for his mother all through his childhood. Sweetie. It bordered on innocuous, but it wasn't something he threw around. He'd never called anyone that.

He had to wait while another paroxysm gripped her. He didn't know how else to soothe her except to hold her and try to absorb her pain and whisper, "I'm worried about *you, søta.*"

Finally, she relaxed and panted, trying to recover before the next wave arrived.

"I'll be there the whole time, Lex. The baby will be safe and so will you. I promise you. I *promise*."

It wasn't something he could promise. He wasn't a surgeon. Things went wrong with childbirth. They'd made that clear in the classes.

She knew it, too. She lifted her head enough to give him a look of weary disillusionment, then her expression crumpled and she caught fistfuls of his shirt and groaned.

The urge to just give the order and make it happen was so strong, he had to lock his throat against it. She would never forgive him if he took this choice from her. Never.

So he waited until the contraction eased and she panted once again. Then he petted her sweaty hair and said, "Please, *søta*. Trust me. I know that's hard, but I won't let anything bad happen to you or the baby. We'll both be here when you wake up. I swear on my life. Trust *me*."

When the next contraction hit, she didn't stiffen. She collapsed into weeping.

"Okay," she sobbed.

"I can order the surgery?" He made her look at him.

Her eyes were streaming, her mouth trembling. She nodded, then ducked her head in defeat.

"It will be okay, *søta*. I swear it." God, he hoped he was telling her the truth.

He called out and the midwife hurried in.

Moments later, they had her on the bed and began preparing her.

"I feel like I'm failing," she said miserably.

"Don't you dare." Magnus braced himself over her. This beautiful fighter had waited for him. He knew that, deep in his heart. It humbled him. He swooped to give her one kiss before he was asked to step back and suit up in scrubs. Then he held her hand, walking beside the gurney as they wheeled her into the theater.

She didn't want the spinal block. She chose full anesthetic, but he was allowed to stay with her because he had damned well promised her he would. They would have to tranquilize him to get him to let go of her hand.

When it went limp in his, his breaths turned shallow. The next forty-eight minutes were the longest of his life.

He didn't watch the procedure. He watched her still face, torn between relief that she was no longer in pain and anguish over what she was going through. Because of him.

Then a squawk sounded behind the drape.

"A boy, Your Highness. A big one," the doctor said with a chuckle of wonder. "Do you want to cut the cord?"

His hand shook. The angry face of his son squinted at him. Magnus's vision blurred.

"Put him here. She wanted skin contact," Magnus insisted in an unsteady voice. He unbuttoned the top of her nightgown enough that the infant could rest on her chest while the midwife covered the baby in a warmed towel and gently dried him.

Magnus only realized he had picked up Lexi's hand again when the midwife asked if he wanted to hold his son.

The baby complained when he was taken from Lexi and loosely swaddled. He didn't want to be separated from his mama, but as Magnus took him into the crook of his arm, the buzzing arrived in his ears again.

"Is Lexi okay?" Magnus asked, mind split in two directions.

"It's going very well, sir. We're finishing up."

Magnus could hardly hear him, the buzz in his ears was so deafening. It filled him with a vibration that made him afraid he would drop this creature who blinked and looked so earnestly into his eyes. For some reason, Magnus wanted to laugh. It was an urge the likes of which he hadn't experienced since childhood.

"If you let me weigh him, sir, he can go with you into recovery with the princess."

"I don't want to let him go," he admitted. But he let the midwife take the baby and he picked up Lexi's hand again, holding on to her while he watched over her and their son.

Lexi slowly became aware of Magnus's voice. He was talking to someone in Isleifisch. He sounded...

She turned her head, still foggy.

"Why are you talking to a towel?" she asked.

"You see?" He tilted the rolled towel. "I told you she would wake soon."

"Oh," she sighed. One clumsy hand went to the bandage on her abdomen, where she felt weak and sore and empty. The other lifted, trying to reach the ruddy face scowling from the swaddle.

"Look at this young man you made." Magnus settled the baby half on her chest, so she could secure him with her arm and see his face. "Ten pounds, ten ounces. I made them convert it so you would know how big he was."

"Hello, Rolf," she said, smiling and touching his round little cheek.

Magnus gave a small exhale of exasperation and set his hand on the top of her head. His thumb caressed her brow.

"Since I witnessed what you had to endure, I will allow you to call our son Rolf Thorolf. But his given name will be Eryk and that is the name we will tell the queen." He kissed her brow. "I'm hoping you're still goofy from the anesthetic and won't remember I said that."

Maybe she was goofy from the anesthetic because she said, "I was afraid someone would take him while I was asleep, and he wouldn't be here when I woke up."

Magnus flinched and covered the hand that cradled their son. "I know. But I promised you that we would both be here, Lex, and I meant it. You can trust me now. Hmm?"

She nodded, starting to believe it.

CHAPTER ELEVEN

WHAT LEXI REALIZED over the next weeks was that trusting her husband meant she began to trust him with her heart. She was falling in love with him.

At first, she thought it was a side effect of the love she felt for her son. She was utterly enraptured with Prince Eryk Rolf Alexander Thorolf. He cried loud, consumed gallons and slept hard. He had fine blond hair and piercing blue eyes and smiled when he dreamed. He had two doting and underworked nannies because Lexi liked to keep him where she could see him.

She especially loved seeing him with his father.

That's when she began to recognize what was happening to her. Magnus would show up in the middle of the day and say, "I only have a minute before my next meeting, but I wanted to see what sort of trouble you two were getting into."

It was never more dramatic than nursing or snuggling while she read a book, but Magnus would kiss her and steal Rolf from her arms and tell him state secrets in Isleifisch before he handed him back and kissed her again.

She would just *melt* through those hit-and-run moments of affection, then she would begin counting the minutes until he came back for the evening.

Almost from the first night they had brought him home, after Rolf was bathed and fed, Magnus would take him to see the queen.

Lexi half suspected Magnus did it so she would get used to trusting that it was safe to let her baby out of her sight for a half hour. It caused her the normal amount of new-mother anxiety, but she also knew that her son needed to bond with his aunt, since Katla would provide him guidance on the role he would one day assume.

One evening, Magnus hadn't turned up by the time Rolf usually went up so Lexi took him. She was still recovering from her surgery, so she was moving slowly.

"You carried him up the stairs yourself?" Katla scolded. "Why didn't you take the pram and the elevator?"

Because that was an even longer walk, but Lexi didn't say so.

"Do not set back your recovery, Lexi. You need to attend that summit in New York with Magnus next month. Otherwise, your countrymen will think we're holding you hostage." She held Rolf aloft. "You're such a big, strong boy, aren't you?"

Lexi took her at her word. A few nights later, Magnus swept into their suite muttering impatiently, "These people who don't know how to end a meeting without telling you what they've already said." He looked around. "Where is he?"

"I sent him up." She set aside the book she was reading.

"Is he walking already? They really do grow up fast."

He picked up her feet and sat, then set her feet in his lap, exactly as he had done so often while she'd been pregnant.

"Ulmer said that since we'll be in New York over American Thanksgiving, he thinks I should host a charity dinner." She wrinkled her nose. "At first, I thought he meant serving meals at a soup kitchen, which I'm happy to do, but he means putting on a whole…thing."

"Why are you reluctant?"

"I was hoping I could stay here in the palace. Maybe never go outside again?"

"Ah. Well, I thought I could finally have someone prettier than Ulmer standing beside me while I make all my appearances."

"It's a tight race," she said with a grimace. "I'm not feeling very pretty."

"Why the hell not? Because I'm not crawling all over you, telling you how irresistible you are?" In a swift move, he was between her legs, wide hands easily dragging her hips down the sofa so he could loom over her and plant a long, lazy kiss on her mouth.

She caught her breath in surprise, then relaxed into the kiss, letting her leg curl around his waist. Her arms twined around his shoulders and she burrowed her fingers beneath the binding on his hair, looking for the heat of his neck.

"This sex ban is torture." He nipped lightly at her chin. "How are you not aware that I'm ogling your breasts at every opportunity? You are very, very beautiful, goddess. Let me show you off."

"People will judge," she said in a plaintive whisper,

stroking his beard. "I didn't care before. Well, I did." It had hurt like hell. "But it was only me they were judging so I could stand it. Now they'll judge you for marrying me. It doesn't matter if I make a mistake or not, they'll find one and everything I do will reflect on you and Rolf."

"It will," he agreed in his no-nonsense way that always seemed to pull the rug on her. "But you are such a fierce warrior behind this angelic face of yours." He swept his fingertip along her brow and down her cheek. "I know that you'll slay them in your sly, ruthless way."

"What is that supposed to mean?" She pushed at his shoulder.

"Oh, please. You win people over with laser-focused charm. Even Ulmer has started to hyperventilate if he risks disappointing you. 'The princess will be waiting, sir,'" he mocked. "I caught the cook having a little cry because you gave her some things to send to her niece for her birthday. How did you even know it was her niece's birthday?"

"We were chatting. She's a fan of Paisley Pocket. I was being nice, not manipulative."

"I know. I'm not insulting you. It's a *strength*. That's why I want you by my side, Lexi. I'm proud of you. I like being out with you."

His words went into her like the sweetest blade, pushing tears into her eyes. Did he really say he was *proud* of her?

Magnus didn't say anything he didn't mean. She'd learned that much about him.

They kissed again and she clung to his shoulders, thinking, *I'm falling. This is what it means to fall in love.*

It was a visceral sensation that was both beautiful and terrifying. In another world, falling in love with her husband would be ideal, but as she regained her physical strength, she was losing the battle to keep her heart.

Did she need to guard it, though? Magnus was incredibly protective of her. As they began making appearances across Isleif, the slightest overstep by anyone was glared into apologies by her ferocious husband.

That was the real reason people fell over themselves to please her, she suspected wryly. But his defense of her built her confidence in their marriage and herself.

By the time they landed in New York, she had almost convinced herself she was not that old person the trolls loved to vilify.

They arrived to a crowd rabid with excitement and a friendly press conference that was mostly photos. Lexi did one softball interview with a morning show where she talked about being a new mother. Rolf made a brief appearance, sending the studio audience into coos of adoration. Being his father's son, Rolf scowled once at the lights and cameras, then ignored them in favor of rooting for her breast.

Lexi then attended a handful of meet-and-greets with Magnus, shaking hands with the president. She spent a couple of hours helping serve lunch at a shelter and visited children in a hospital.

High on her success, she came into their hotel bedroom to find Magnus undressing for his shower. She was in her robe, having just showered herself, since they were expected at a mixer this evening.

"I just did something scary."

"What's that?" He pulled off his belt and threw it on the chair.

"I told the nanny that we'll be out for several hours tomorrow, so I think we should have a small rehearsal. I pumped two bottles and told her to see if Rolf will take one when he wakes. Then I said I was going to rest for an hour and not to disturb me."

Magnus slid his gaze to the bed, then the clock on the table beside it.

"You're invited," she clarified. "In case you didn't know what day it is."

"I can count," he assured her as he padded toward her.

When his hand came out, she thought he was going to scoop her around the waist and drag her into him, but he turned the lock on the door behind her.

Then he used both hands to wrench open the robe, throwing it to the floor and leaving her naked and cutting off her scream of shock. She slapped her hand over her mouth, laughing, certain the staff would hear her, but he was already picking her up so her legs had to wind around his waist while he walked her to the bed and came down on top of her.

"I will make every single one of the next sixty minutes count," he promised as he dragged his mouth to her throat and left a wet kiss there.

"The doctor said it might be uncomfortable. I might need lube. There's some in my makeup bag." She looked toward the bathroom.

"I'll fetch it if we need it." He looked up from circling his tongue on her distended nipple, then reached between them to tear her underwear away, leaving a small friction burn near her hip. "But we never have before, have we?"

And down his mouth went, pausing to skim lightly over the numb line of her scar before he parted her folds and anointed her, preparing her. Driving her to the brink of orgasm within moments, then leaving her panting and whimpering in loss as he stood to tear off his own clothes.

When he came back down on her, she opened arms and legs to welcome him. She groaned with delight at the feel of his splayed hand possessing her ass, holding her steady as he carefully forged into her. She bit her lip, experiencing a virgin-like sting, but reveling in it because his nostrils were flaring and his eyes were blazing and he shook with the effort to hold on to his control.

She loved him, she acknowledged as a brilliant glow filled her. She loved this man who claimed her, groaning in helpless need, and folded himself across her.

This was the man she had met in Paris, the one who consumed her, but it was also the man who had come to know that she liked a caress in her lower back while they made love. One who knew he could rise on his knees and arch her over his arm and tell her to make herself come so he could feel it. One who held back so he could arouse her again and again, tipping her over the edge and picking her up until she was glassy-eyed with sexual excess, utterly his.

Then he unleashed himself, letting his shout of gratification fill the room.

And, because they still had eleven minutes, he dragged her into the shower where he gently soaped her and set tender kisses on her heavy eyelids and told her she was too sexy for words and that she would be his downfall.

She laughed, drunk on eroticism, but that word—downfall—came back to her later, haunting her.

CHAPTER TWELVE

As far as Magnus was concerned, he and his small family had conquered America. Their Thanksgiving-themed fundraiser had raised several million dollars for meals for underprivileged families. Lexi had been the belle of the ball in a sequin-covered creation of reds and golds like autumn leaves. Her profile lifted Isleif's and this time when they danced, they received applause.

They had earned a pseudo-honeymoon as they headed into a quieter December. Lexi was feeling more confident in her role as his wife and was finding a routine of sorts with their son. She was also bouncing back physically so she was very receptive to lovemaking.

A few mornings after their return, Magnus told her to stay in bed after she fed Rolf. He took the boy to their small dining room, burping him while he ate his own breakfast.

Rolf continued to put on weight and was growing stronger every day, holding up his head and pushing his arms and legs with determination, even though he didn't seem to have a destination in mind except to scale Magnus's shoulder. It was an amusing wrestling match, trying to keep a secure hold on him while trying to spread jam on his toast.

"Your Royal Highness." Ulmer paused to give Magnus a polite nod of greeting as he was shown in. "Good morning."

"Why are you here? My morning is free of engagements." Magnus had planned it that way. Once Rolf went down for his nap, he intended to rejoin his wife in their bed.

"Publicity concerns have cropped up." Ulmer swept his finger across his tablet. "I wanted to let you know we're aware of them and addressing them before..." Ulmer glanced toward the open door to the corridor that led to their bedroom. He smiled politely, but his lips were tight. "Good morning, Your Highness."

"Good morning, Ulmer." Lexi had secured a robe over her silk pajamas. It was hardly the first time Ulmer had seen her before she'd dressed, but she faltered. "I thought we had a free morning."

"I thought you were sleeping in?" Magnus countered.

"I'm hungry. Oh, yes, good morning to you, too. As if we haven't already said that." Her voice dropped to a gurgle of indulgence as she smoothed her hand over their son's fine hair. "You can't possibly be hungry, too? You *just* ate, you little glutton."

Hungry or not, Rolf wiggled harder, always aware when his mama was near and eager to be in her arms.

She took him and sat in the chair Ulmer held for her. Magnus moved his toast to where she could reach it and held up two fingers for the poached eggs she usually ate. Their server poured her decaf coffee and left.

"You were saying something about publicity concerns?" Lexi prompted Ulmer. "About me? I'm guessing it's not good."

"We're well aware that controversy sells clicks, ma'am. We're doing what we can to quash it, but they are being persistent."

"What are they saying?" Her voice was even, but Magnus heard the dread.

Ulmer looked as though he'd allow himself to be drawn and quartered before he repeated any of it.

"It doesn't matter," Magnus stated. "The staff are dealing with it so you don't have to. Carry on," he said, dismissing the man.

But later, after they'd made love and were sharing a lazy bath, he heard her "Tsk." He picked up his head off the back of the tub and found her reading headlines on a phone he didn't recognize.

"What are you doing? Where did you get this?" He took it from her, noting it was in a waterproof case.

"It's the one I keep in here for reading while I'm in the tub."

"Then read a book, not that garbage." He tossed it to the mat on the floor.

"They're saying I should have lost the baby weight by now."

"It's all in your chest. I think it's delightful." He slid his hand under the water so he could weigh the swell that overflowed his palm.

She didn't relax into him the way he'd hoped. "They think I'm lazy because I had a C-section instead of delivering naturally."

"'They' don't exist. One troll in the armpit of the internet is trying to profit off you. Are you really going to let them ruin our morning?"

"No," she said petulantly.

But it did cast a shadow, one that grew longer and darker as the month wore on.

Magnus didn't tell her that her post-pregnancy photos were being compared to ones that her stalker had posted a few years ago, but he had a suspicion she knew. She grew subdued while he grew frustrated. He had sworn she could rely on him to look after her, hadn't he? Why couldn't he protect her from something that caused her so much pain?

On Christmas day, he had his own history to face and thank God Lexi and Rolf were there to buffer him through it. Every few years, he had Christmas lunch at the cottage with his mother. This year, everyone was there, including Sveyn.

Snow was falling heavily. The sun had barely come up before it began to set, casting the day in a muted light. The babies were being passed around like plates of hors d'oeuvres and the women were caught up in lively conversation about sleep schedules and baby yoga.

When Freyr tilted his head at Magnus and said, "Sauna?" Magnus hesitated, not wanting to leave Lexi alone, but sitting in the sauna was something they had done throughout his childhood, boys and girls taking turns in the hut built for that purpose. He was here to take Rolf if Lexi and the women wanted to steam together later.

It was a setup, of course. He was no sooner seated

on the top bench, sweating onto his towel, when Freyr invented a need to stoke the fire and took their brother-in-law with him, leaving Magnus with Sveyn.

Biting back a curse, Magnus demanded, "What is it?"

There was a weighty, indrawn breath, then, "I want to ask your mother to marry me."

"You don't need my permission."

"But I want your blessing."

Magnus stared balefully at his father through the billows of steam. Sveyn had aged. That was the thought that recurred each time he'd seen him lately. He worked in insurance, but his hobbies had always been outdoor pastimes. He was still fit and lean, but now his shoulders were bony, his face deeply lined, his red beard heavily salted with white.

"I want your forgiveness," Sveyn admitted with emotion in his voice. "That is what I really want to ask you. It took me a long time, Magnus. Too long to realize this wasn't about me or what I thought our life should have been. Nothing was stolen from me that I didn't let go of through spite. I wish I could go back and fight for more time with you, but I can't. I'm sorry for that. Truly."

Magnus believed him and, really, what was the point in holding a grudge now?

"I was an adult. I made the decision to come here. I'm glad you're no longer punishing Mom for my actions."

"You didn't make a decision," Sveyn said with ire. "You made a sacrifice. So did she. It took me far too long to understand that. To accept that it was her right to decide—I couldn't fathom how she could carry any man's baby but mine, especially—" He gave an agitated rub of his beard. "Especially when she knew it didn't matter how much she loved you, she might have to give you up. It felt as though she made all of those decisions without me. Even though they affected me. I wanted to keep everything as it was. I wanted to keep my *son*. For myself. But I know now that was selfish of me. Incredibly selfish."

A skewer invaded Magnus's chest, making his breath burn. He told himself it was the scald of the hot, humid air, but it was the score of that word: *selfish*.

She knew it didn't matter how much she loved you, she might have to give you up.

"Can you forgive me?" His father's voice came from far away.

"Yes." He cleared his throat. "Of course." Because *he* was not a selfish man. Was he?

"Thank you, son." His father's hand came out and Magnus leaned forward to shake it, thinking this should have felt more healing, but those words—*sacrifice* and *selfish*—glinted like two sides of a coin tumbling through the clouds of steam.

For Christmas, Dalla had given Lexi tickets to a play in London starring her former Paisley Pockets costar, Josh, who had played her onscreen brother. Dalla had checked with Magnus beforehand and he had suggested booking the New Year's Eve performance, so they could watch the fireworks afterward.

"I haven't seen you in such a good mood in weeks," Magnus said as Lexi pulled on black palazzo pants shot with gold threads that glinted as she moved.

"I haven't seen Josh in years. We used to text, but... life." She shrugged on the matching jacket over a gold push-up bra. "Thank you for bringing me." She looped her arms around his back.

"It was Dalla's idea."

"I know, but you agreed, even though the paps will be a nightmare about it." Those awful nudes of hers that Carmichael had peddled had been churned up along with comments that she was "poisoning" the royal line and turning Prince Magnus into his father. No matter what she did, she couldn't seem to burn away that old reputation and rise above it, which left her feeling guilty and ashamed for exposing her husband and child to the same ridicule.

"How many times do I have to tell you I don't care what the press says about you?" He set her back and slid his gaze down her front. "Anyone with eyes will say you look stunning."

"Thank you." She appreciated the compliment, but he didn't kiss her or try to distract her. He'd been growing more and more withdrawn lately and it was starting to distress her.

"We should go. The play will start whether we arrive on time or not. I'm guessing you don't want to miss any of it."

She didn't, but she also didn't like this feeling that he might *say* he didn't care about her reputation, but she couldn't fully believe him because her reputation had been an issue from the very beginning. A lifetime in an industry of broken promises and last-minute rejections had trained her to be skeptical and to expect to be cut adrift at any moment.

She wanted to believe her husband when he told her it didn't matter. In many ways, she was living her best life with him. She loved Magnus, loved their son. She wanted to tell Magnus that and celebrate this wonderful life they were making together, but each time he pulled away that little bit, she lost her nerve, feeling insecure and uncertain.

She trusted him with her life, but she didn't have enough trust in his feelings toward her to risk her own.

Her brooding thoughts were set aside for ninety minutes while they watched the play, a mystery that was suspenseful enough to silence the audience for long minutes at a time. When it concluded, Lexi was the first to leap to her feet, clapping wildly for Josh and the rest of the talented cast.

She had sent a note backstage when they arrived, telling Josh to break a leg, as if their presence in the audience wouldn't have been noted otherwise. They had been a distraction on and off throughout, but they were escorted backstage where they were greeted with great excitement.

After a small gauntlet of handshaking, they entered Josh's dressing room and Lexi flew into the arms of her old friend.

"You jerk," Josh grumbled as he squeezed her. "You made me so nervous, knowing you were in the audience." He had his hair dyed red for his role and wore traces of his stage makeup, but he gave her a second hug, picking her up and crushing her like a long-lost relative.

"You were amazing," she assured him. "But put me down so I can introduce you to Magnus."

"Excellent performance," Magnus said politely as he shook Josh's hand.

"A far cry from pretending to pick you out of garbage disposals, isn't it?" Josh joked to Lexi. "Ooh, let's start rumors of a reboot." He pulled his phone from his robe pocket.

"Wait. Let me do it on mine." Lexi wrinkled her nose. "Magnus has to be in it or the trolls will claim I'm having an affair."

"Please. I'm out and proud these days, Lex. If anything, they'll think I'm after your husband. Oh! Come to our party tonight! Meet my partner, David. You'll know so many people. I'm *dying* to hear why you left X-Calibur. And you have a *baby*?"

"We do have a son and we have to get back to him," she said smoothly. "But here. Magnus will take the photo and I'll send it to you. Post it whenever you want, but *please* say something boring. You have no idea what I'm going through."

"Babe, I was outed by a podcast host so they could boost their ratings. I have some idea." Josh slid his arm around her waist and tilted his head against hers, smiling wide as Magnus used his long arm to snap the photo of the three of them. "Did you really drop out of the project with Bernadette Garnier? It's *Bernadette Garnier*, Lex. And that role would be perfect for you."

"I know, but…" Lexi shrugged that off as she glanced at the photo, then asked for Josh's number so she could send it to him. "Even funding it is an issue. I believe in the story, but the trolls are finding the topic too darned salacious. Guard my number with your life, please. Otherwise, I'll have to change it and we'll lose touch again."

"I will. *I miss you.*" He hugged her again.

She kissed his cheek and they said their goodbyes.

When they were in the car, Magnus asked, "Text him for the address if you want to go to the party. I don't mind."

"It's not worth it. The trolls will turn it into me abandoning our son and accuse me of falling back into drugs or something."

"Lexi. You can't keep living around what strangers are saying about you, especially when it's said in bad faith. If you want to see your friend, do it. If you want to keep a foot in acting, let's talk about how to make that happen."

"I don't." She looked to him with puzzlement. "That part of my life is over."

"What part? The happy part?"

"I'm happy," she defended.

"Don't lie to me," he snapped.

They didn't speak again until they were back in their suite at the hotel on the Thames. Rolf was down for the night so Lexi took the baby monitor and dismissed the nanny.

"Why do you think I'm not happy?" she asked as they changed from their evening wear.

"Because you looked happy tonight in a way I haven't seen in weeks. Or were you *acting* happy? Because it was either him or being around actors that made you light up like that. If it's acting, and you want to go back to it, then we should talk about it."

And add bad reviews to her already full plate of negative feedback?

"Josh and I grew up together. He's like a brother to me. But he's always been gay, Magnus. If you think there's something between us—"

"I'm not jealous," he said pithily.

Ouch.

"Good," she claimed. "Because you don't have any reason to be."

"But I can't be your whole life," he added.

"You're not. Rolf is." She was stooping to being mean, but he was standing right on her heart.

They glared at each other, but she looked away first.

"Do you *want* me to go back to acting?" she asked with trepidation. Was this his way of pushing her out of his life now that she'd produced the heir he needed?

"I don't want the guilt of keeping you from something you love."

"You're not. I'm making a choice."

"You're making a sacrifice."

"For my *son*."

"Exactly."

"I don't even know what we're fighting about," she muttered, leaving her couture clothes on the floor and yanking to tie the belt on her robe.

"We're fighting about the fact that I stole your life from you."

"What life?" she cried. "I chose to have him, Magnus. Not because I wanted to be the mother of a king, but because I wanted to be a *mother*. This is not the way I imagined my life would turn out, that's true, but it's a very good life. I—" Oh, she would have to say it. "I'm in this life because I love you."

"Don't say that." He winced and looked away.

He might as well have knocked her off the top of the building into the Thames. She sucked in a breath, unable to find words.

"Lex—"

"No," she choked, holding up a hand. "*Now* you've given me a reason to look for fulfillment elsewhere."

"Let me explain what I meant," he said tightly.

"Do you love me?" she demanded.

He hesitated and his expression became that stony horrible one that gave away nothing, which finished crushing her heart.

On the monitor, Rolf began to fuss. She snatched it up and headed for the door, thankful that she wouldn't complete her humiliation by crying in front of Magnus.

He could have called out to her, though. He could have told her to ask the nanny to get their son and stay here to work this out.

He could have fought for her.

But he didn't.

He let her walk out.

And she was devastated.

He shouldn't have let her walk out. He should have said, *Yes. I love you. I love you in ways I didn't know I could love.*

Because he did. And it made him feel as though he was being boiled alive.

From the time Sveyn had talked to him about sacrifice and selfishness, Magnus could only see himself as selfish where Lexi was concerned. He had wanted her from the moment he spotted her. He had balked at being told he couldn't have her and had found a way to stay in the periphery of her life even when he shouldn't have. The very second that he'd had an excuse to drag her into his world, he'd acted ruthlessly to do so.

And he'd been watching her suffer for it the whole time. She might have chosen to carry the pregnancy and become a mother, but she hadn't wanted the strictures of royal life. She had known their marriage would make her that much more of a target of attention, especially the negative kind.

Magnus had countered all of those downsides with his own rationalizations. He protected her. He supported her and the child they'd made. He gave her as much physical pleasure as they could bear. He had given her a family, such as his was, to replace the one he'd cost her by exposing their treachery.

Then, tonight, Magnus had seen for the first time that she did have a family she loved. A life where she was welcomed and celebrated. Her childhood friend had put carefree laughter into her eyes, if only for a few moments.

A ferocious tightening had sat in his chest while Magnus had watched them. Their connection had been similar to the way Freyr still hugged Dalla sometimes. It had struck Magnus as too similar. Had he broken her away from a place where she felt loved and accepted? Why? So she could live inside the boundaries of his life and still suffer the anguish of what strangers said about her?

When she asked if he loved her, he couldn't see how telling her would help. It wouldn't change anything. It would only make her feel obligated to accept this life he'd forced her to take on.

That's why he'd told her not to say it. If she loved him, it meant she would keep making sacrifices for him. He didn't want that from her. He wanted her to thrive. He wanted her to be the delightful force he knew her to be, with her strong personality and her cheeky remarks and her way of leading with her heart no matter how many times she'd been disappointed by those around her.

How could she even say she loved him? That was the real reason he'd told her not to say it. How could she love him after the things he'd done to cage her into this life with him? He'd done it out of selfishness, because he was so damned tired of being alone. How could she love *that*?

She didn't come to their bed, staying in Rolf's room overnight. She didn't talk much the next morning either, keeping the baby and nannies and Ulmer between them as a buffer.

When they arrived back on Isleif, she said she had a headache so Magnus let her retreat to her room while he brooded on how he would pull them from this tailspin.

Before he saw Lexi the following morning, he was summoned to speak to Katla.

Irritated by what felt like a prime example of what had caused their fight—the fact that his obligation to the crown would always come before her—he strode into the formal receiving room with his usual flouting of protocol.

"Is this about Asia? I've already had discussions with Sorr. It's under control."

"No. That trip will be canceled. We have a personal matter to discuss."

"You are not going to attack me about Lexi. She's all but living under a veil. No, Katla. We have to learn to live with the bad press."

"Magnus," she said with quiet urgency. "I've been waiting until the diagnosis was confirmed. I have the same heart defect as my mother. I must abdicate."

CHAPTER THIRTEEN

THE WORLD FLIPPED on its axis.

No, he thought.

"Yes, Magnus," she said, making him realize he'd spoken his reaction aloud.

"It's really that serious?" The severity of this news—of her condition—drove him to his knee before her.

"Have you known me to be overly dramatic?" There were lines of distress around her eyes. Her lips were pale. "It's not as severe as hers, but I've been struggling to breathe lately. I can't continue with my duties, but with careful management, I should have a few years before I require a transplant."

"A transplant." That punched the air out of him.

"I'm being brutally honest with you, which I know is one of the things you hate most about me, but it's necessary."

"I don't hate you. I find your desire to do the right thing extremely annoying." He let himself fall onto his ass, turning as he did so his back landed against the chair that was angled toward hers. He braced his wrist on his upraised knee, trying to take it in.

"I don't want you to be ill." It was an understatement,

but it was the most emotion he could allow himself to express without giving in to the shaken sensation in his chest. He and Katla clashed because they were knitted from the same chain-link armor, but she was as much his sibling as Dalla or Freyr. It would break his heart to lose her.

"I don't wish to be ill either, but it is a fact so we'll deal with it," she said with her own steely refusal to give in to emotion.

They would deal with it, but he had time to process what her illness meant to both of them. To help her find the care she needed to prolong her life, but the other part. King? He'd been preparing nearly fifteen years, but it still seemed like a bizarre fantasy so he brushed that aside to be parsed through in the coming hours and days.

No, in this moment, his most immediate concern was, "What do I do about Lexi?"

"What do you mean?"

"Come on, Katla. Look what I've done to her, forcing her into royal life the way you did to me. At least I had the DNA. What you did was necessary, but I essentially kidnapped her." There'd even been a level of emotional extortion when she had tried to delay their marriage and he'd challenged her on what kind of woman she was. He pinched the bridge of his nose, remembering their most recent argument. "When we were in London, I told her she should go back to acting if she wants to. Now I have to go walk that back? Tell her she has to stay here and become queen? I'd best have one of the bodyguards in the room with me. She's liable to kill me."

"Why on earth would you tell her to go back to acting?" Katla cried. "She's a perfect partner for you. She makes you *better*, Magnus."

"She makes me selfish," he argued, thrusting to his feet. "You know that. I could have made arrangements for her, let her raise Rolf away from all of this."

His chest felt ripped open at the thought. His son had become a part of him, but he shook off the sensation. At the time, his son hadn't been real to him. It had all been about Lexi. About his desire to drag her into his life.

"I wanted her and went around you to get her. But the weight of this is affecting her. I don't want to crush her and lose her. I love her too much to watch that happen."

"I know you do," Katla said with a choke of humorless laughter. "That's been obvious to me since I heard the defiance in your voice when you told me she was pregnant. You were so glad. So proud. It was—" She looked away and blinked.

"Katla." The unfairness of her infertility hit him anew.

"I do strive to do what's right." She folded her hands in her lap, gaze pensively fixed on the ring she wore. "I think often that if I'd been able to have children, I would not have had to force you to take this on. It was deeply unfair to you and your mother and your whole family. Sometimes there is no clear path that is wholly right, Magnus."

"I know, but…" He ran his hand over his face. "But what you have demonstrated to me again and again, what I know to be true, is that this is a life where my wants and needs are second to the greater good. How can I be good enough to take the crown if I don't have the strength of character to give her up, if that's what is right for *her*?"

He had to look away, to hide the fact that his eyes were growing damp. His chest was tight and there was a deep ache behind his sternum, one so acute it felt like a fracture.

"Oh, Magnus, I hope you know I'm not a saint. Look at this choice I'm making right now. Is it not selfish of me that I would rather step back from my duties in hopes of living longer?"

"*I* want that." He pointed to his chest. "I would rather you were here to provide advice than leave me to face this without you. Another self-serving act," he muttered with a derisive wave at himself.

"And I want to live so I may see you rule," she said quietly. In a rare moment of humanity, she let her mask slip and he saw affection and chagrin and humility. "I know you will rise to it, Magnus. You will make a wonderful king. I am so proud of you. I can't bear not to witness it."

Ah, hell. She was going to make him cry.

"When?" His voice thickened with emotion, because this wasn't a choice. It was his destiny.

"A month?"

He nodded, accepting it, but all he could think was, *What about Lexi?*

Lexi was very used to rejection. For every role she'd landed, she'd been turned down for dozens more. For every comment or post that called her a fashion icon or a "Mom Worth Modeling" there were a hundred others that tore her down.

She knew that you couldn't win if you didn't try, and that trying meant risking failure, but that was what was smothering her right now: a sense of failure.

She had risked her heart and the man she loved didn't love her back. She was married to him. They had a son—one who would one day be king of this country she had grown to love. She wanted to make Rolf proud. She wanted to make *Magnus* proud.

And she was failing.

She did the only thing she could do. She dismissed the nanny and cuddled her baby, soaking up Rolf's chubby warmth and the feel of his fingers curling into her shirt, his kicking legs and his wet mouth bapping her cheek.

"Lex?" Magnus came into their lounge, voice and expression grave enough to tighten her stomach. "We need to talk."

"Magnus, it's fine," she insisted while drowning in defensiveness and a desire to quickly move back to what they'd had while also wondering if that was even possible. "I knew love was not something you were offering when we married. I didn't mean to make you feel obligated."

"It's not fine. But I'd rather we weren't distracted." He rang for the nanny.

She closed her arms more firmly around Rolf. "You know he can't speak English any better than Isleifisch, right?"

Not one hint of amusement. Magnus was somber as

he told the nanny they had some important matters to discuss and didn't want to be disturbed.

Lexi's heart lurched and she was reluctant to give Rolf up. Her arms felt empty as she followed Magnus into his office. Her chest ached with a chill of apprehension.

"Magnus—" She didn't even know what to say, she only knew that whatever he was planning to say would hurt.

"I need to tell you first that we're not going to Asia. Katla is ill. She's planning to abdicate within the next few weeks."

Lexi's shock was so great her mind blanked for several seconds.

"I know," he said, guiding her toward a chair. "Sit. It's a lot to take in."

"But… *How* ill? Magnus…" She searched his expression as she sank onto the cushion. Her stomach twisted into knots when she saw the shadows of worry behind his eyes.

"It's a heart condition similar to her mother's. If she reduces stress and makes resting a priority, she should be with us for a good while." It wasn't even lunch, but he poured himself a drink, then left it on a side table as he sat down to face her.

"She seems so young," Lexi said, voice coming out hushed because there was no wind in her. "Obviously, I knew you would become king eventually, but that felt like something that would happen years from now. I don't know what to say."

"Say you'll stay."

"What?" She lifted her head, only then realizing she

had buried her face in her hands. "Of course I'll stay. I told you, I don't want to go back to acting. I want to—" She swallowed. "I want to be Rolf's mother."

"And my wife? My queen?" His expression flexed with some unnamed emotion. "Say you love me again."

Her mouth clamped reflexively into a hard line.

"Let me respond properly this time." He hitched forward in his seat and extended his hand.

"I don't want you to say something you don't mean." She bit her lips, trying to steady them. "I meant it when I said it's fine. I'll stay. You'll have more responsibilities and won't have as much flexibility for Rolf. It wouldn't be a good look for me to choose now to pursue my own interests. If you can stand my reputation, I'll take on the role of queen."

"You won't say it?" he asked grittily. "I killed those feelings in you? You are not that fickle." He rose and pointed at her, staring down his nose at her. "Fine. Don't say it. I told you not to say it because I didn't feel I deserved to hear it. I still don't." He turned his back on her.

"Oh, do you have some horrible nude photos that the internet keeps regurgitating?" she asked scathingly.

"That." He gave his beard a scrub as he turned to face her, pointing again. "That is one of the reasons I don't deserve your love. I can't make all that poison go away no matter how hard I try. I make it worse. Being my wife makes all of that worse for you." He exhaled, sounding exhausted, and dropped his hands to his sides. "When I talked to my father on Christmas Day, he told me he held on to his anger for so long because he hadn't had any choice in what had happened. That he felt my mother had made all his choices for him. When he said that, I realized that I hadn't given you a choice. At first, I was able to believe I was justified, but you haven't been happy, Lexi."

"Because I could tell *you* weren't happy. I thought it was because of all the bad press."

"I'm going to say this one last time." He closed his eyes and tilted his head to the ceiling. "Then we will never talk about it again. *Screw the press.* They can all go to hell. I know who you are, Lexi. And I love you. Exactly as you are."

Love was an arrow. It went into her chest with the sweetest burn, sitting there vibrating and stinging, putting tears into her eyes.

She hugged herself, voice a thin rattle. "Do you really?"

"Yes, damn you." His expression turned so tender, it broke her all over again. "I think it started in Paris, when you asked who was in charge. You knew damned well it was me. And you will never know how hard it was for me to say no to you in Monte Carlo."

"It was hard for me to ask," she muttered with a pang of remembered hurt.

"I know. And I will always be angry with myself for giving up that time I could have had with you, but I didn't know then how much you meant to me. I didn't really understand it until Rolf's birth. Everything about that day scared me, Lexi, especially when I realized I could lose you. I didn't want to face what that meant, though. I didn't accept how much I loved you until you accused me of being jealous of a gay man whom you think of as a brother and I was."

"You said you weren't!"

"I lied. I won't do it again," he promised, running his hand down his face and tugging at his beard. "But he made you smile in a way I hadn't seen in weeks. I couldn't stand that he could give you that and I didn't."

"It was nostalgia, Magnus. I didn't have a care in the world back then. We were children. You give me other things that are more important than candy bars stolen from craft services."

"Orgasms?" he scoffed.

"Our son. An identity that has substance. The power to affect lives."

"The weight of responsibility," he countered. "Duty. Expectations that are difficult to live up to."

"All true, but were you serious?" She rose and moved toward him, feeling as though she inched onto a plank over an abyss. "Do you love me? Have you given me your heart?"

"Yes," he said promptly. "It's all yours, Lexi. If you're not with me, then I don't have one." He cupped her face, looking into her eyes with such swirls of emotion in his that she felt lifted off the floor and plunged into a whirlpool at the same time. "Will you say it again?"

"I love you, Magnus. I love *you*. The man and the father and the king."

"You'll be my queen."

"I would be honored."

For a few seconds, his mask was completely gone and all she saw was love. So much love it should have frightened her. But the swell of her love for him was so great, it met and matched his, melding into something greater than both of them combined.

When he kissed her, it tasted as reverent and holy as renewing their vows. It was tender and loving and sweet. Eternal.

Then, because they were Magnus and Lexi, she tipped back her head, wrapped her arms around his neck and encouraged him to plunder.

He groaned and angled his head, then slid his hands down to her ass, picking her up so she wrapped her legs around his waist.

"How much time do we have?" he asked against her cheek.

"You told her not to disturb us. There's enough milk in the freezer to buy us a few hours."

"I should show more finesse," he said as he cleared his desk with a sweep of his arm and pressed her back onto it. "But I hate fighting with you. I need to *feel* you, to know we're okay."

They barely undressed. Her slacks were thrown over a chair and her underwear was still dangling off her ankle when she hugged his ribs with her knees.

His entry stung. She wasn't completely ready for him, but he paused and kissed his apology onto the tip of her nose.

"I'm rushing you."

"It's makeup sex. I want to feel connected to you." She tugged his hair free of its band so it fell around her face.

He braced on his elbow, fingertips caressing her temple and cheekbone and the corner of her mouth while he seemed to memorize her features.

"I thought I was losing you," he admitted in a whisper. "I lost everyone I loved before and loving them wasn't enough. I need to know I'm giving you enough, Lexi."

"You do." She finished opening his shirt and ran her hands beneath it, mapping his bare shoulders. "I thought this was all we had, but we have so much more now. And it makes this even better."

"It does," he agreed. As he withdrew and returned, a wicked smile curved his lips. "I like watching your eyes haze like that."

"I like how safe you make me feel, even when you're burning down my world." She wrapped her thighs around his waist and arched, inviting the act. The energy of his powerful thrusts.

"I will spend the rest of my life making you sigh like that," he growled.

"Promise," she gasped.

"On my life."

They stopped talking, too caught up in the pleasure they were giving each other. And soon, the inferno engulfed them.

One month later...

Crowds had been pouring into Isleif for days. People of all ages lined the streets from the palace to the parliament building where Magnus would be declared king.

Security forces had been beefed up with help from allies, particularly the ones who were attending the coronation. It would not be a long ceremony, but every detail had been choreographed to the millisecond.

Their car arrived at the end of the red carpet that led into the building. A deafening roar rose around them as they left the car and walked the short distance into the building. Magnus had always been incredibly popular and, here in Isleif at least, Lexi grew more adored by the day.

Inside, cameras broadcast their short procession, flashing to Queen Katla seated with Sorr, holding Rolf who had the good manners to remain soundly asleep. They were flanked by Magnus's family, including his father, and Rhonda, who still wore an expression of astonishment that her daughter was becoming a queen.

After the formal declaration of Magnus as king, they would travel in a slow parade back to the palace for a full day of celebration. There would be a reception for various local dignitaries, a state dinner for the foreign ones and a midnight ball. The day had been declared a national holiday, so events were planned across the country. Every club, arena, pub and local diner would be packed.

"Magnus," Lexi whispered as the prime minister made his opening remarks. "You're shaking." He normally had nerves of steel.

His expression was the contained one that was difficult to read, but he flashed her a glance, allowing her to glimpse what was in his eyes. In his soul.

He leaned close to say in her ear, "I've always dreaded this day because I thought I would have to face it alone.

But I have you." He picked up her hand and kissed the finger that held her wedding band. "Thank you for being here. Today and in my life. I love you."

He was going to make her cry and she'd taken such care with her makeup.

"I love you, too." The clip of her lips shaping those words would become a GIF shared millions of times around the world, but in those moments, they were spoken by a wife to her husband with the utmost sincerity.

Then the prime minister turned to Magnus and recognized them as, "King Magnus of Isfeild and Queen Alexandra."

EPILOGUE

"LEXI," MAGNUS SAID with exasperation as he strode into the royal chambers. "Ulmer just told me you booked us an hour-long meeting to discuss the decor in the royal apartment? We pay people to choose wallpaper. My choice is to not attend meetings that aren't necessary."

They had moved into the monarch suite as soon as Magnus was crowned, but eight months later, they still hadn't changed any of the furnishings. It was all period pieces and beautiful antiques, many of which he'd begun to complain lacked comfort.

But that wasn't exactly why Lexi had blocked out this time.

"It sounds like you're having a good day," she teased.

"I am dying a death of a thousand paper cuts, all caused by bureaucracy." He looked around. "Where's Rolf?"

"Auntie time." Queen Katla had kept her title, but was typically referred to as the Queen Matriarch. For Rolf, she was very much Auntie Katla. She had more time for him these days and absolutely doted on him.

"Oh?"

"Now his interest in wallpaper sharpens," she noted with amusement.

"Furnishings at least." He stalked toward her. "Pick whatever you like, but make it sturdy." As he passed a writing desk, he gave it a wiggle, then swooped to wrap her in his arms, lifting her so she was eye to eye with him. "*Is* this meeting code for sex? Because I think I just developed a fascination with interior design. We might need a weekly appointment to explore color samples."

"I did want a private discussion without alerting staff." She gave his hair band a light tug, which was always a signal they were about to let their hair down.

"I'm listening."

He was not listening. He was burying his mouth in her neck, making it difficult for her to remember what she wanted to say.

"I, um, saw the doctor today."

He picked up his head, blue gaze darkening with concern. "About?"

"About whether it's too early to conceive again. I'd like the kids to be close in age, if possible. He said we could start trying. What do you think?"

"I think that I want my wife to have everything she wants, so we're going to squeeze lovemaking into my busy schedule every single day, if that's what's necessary to make it happen."

She chuckled. "You're willing to make that great sacrifice, are you?"

"My country can spare me." He walked her through to his bedroom, the one that was called his, but that they shared while hers was mostly a dressing room. "In fact,

I would say it is my most solemn duty as king to make at least one more baby with you."

"I've been thinking I might want three. What do you think?"

"I think we'd better start applying ourselves," he said against her smiling lips.

They did. And because they were Magnus and Lexi, and they wanted to give each other everything and more, they welcomed twin girls within the year.

They had another boy two years after that, just for fun.

* * * * *

Did His Highness's Hidden Heir
*leave you wanting more?
Then you're bound to love these other steamy
Dani Collins stories!*

The Baby His Secretary Carries
The Secret of Their Billion-Dollar Baby
Her Billion-Dollar Bump
Marrying the Enemy
Husband for the Holidays

Available now!

HARLEQUIN
Reader Service

Enjoyed your book?

Try the perfect subscription for Romance readers and get more great books like this delivered right to your door.

See why over 10+ million readers have tried Harlequin Reader Service.

Start with a Free Welcome Collection with free books and a gift—valued over $20.

Choose any series in print or ebook.
See website for details and order today:

TryReaderService.com/subscriptions